Tales of the Peacemaker

Through The First Years

Ashley-Lynn Hall

ISBN
978-1-957895-32-1 (Paperback)
978-1-957895-31-4 (eBook)

Table of Contents

Introduction 1

Joining the Mortals 9

Learning 18

Surprises 28

Saving another 33

Slow what you show others 37

Why would a King… 40

Katana 43

A home for a family 45

Fooling others on my strength 47

Ally? 51

Ancient Poem helps 53

Traitors 55

Unicorns and fighting lessons 60

Instant healing/ speed learning 63

Strong fights 64

Conversation with a sea dragon 67

Many fights 69

Questions 70

Punishment 72

Fairy help 76

Blindfolded fights 80

Losing grandpa 83

Challenge 85

Loss of freedom 87

Freedom 97

A princess raised as a slave 101

A princess finds her prince 103

Buying deeds at a high cost 107

Not as you seem 112

Treaty 114

Next generation 116

More known magic 120

Saving a child's life 126

Messages 128

Second temporary union 130

Punishment again 136

Elves 138

The Lights 147

Space and time continuums 149

Spell caster magic 151

Water and fire magic 156

Major loss 158

Give her the last name Peacemaker 160

A child is alone 163

Heading home 166

Introduction

I am Sam. I am an immortal born. Immortals that are born so do not have last names until they choose some and prove they can lead the mortals. Failure gives them their parent's last name and not able to get past their parent's rank at the time they declared desire for a last name. I am sitting with my parents, Zeyla Star and Merk Mer. They are both immortals and watching over some mortals. They are training me on how to look after them. They are watching a mortal dragon prince, named Matt and a mortal mermaid queen named Merth Ann. We see them get married. Minutes later they enter a private space. The view port closes in respect for privacy. I ask, "Are mortals able to handle fire and water mixes?"

Mom replies, "No. They are the couple we intend to place you with so you can choose a last name. Your presence will help her reduce pain when she ends up pregnant. As they are both royals, they will have twins. The no nation left without an heir law comes into effect. Did you see she holds a crystal with the name of the mortal crystal people's ruler carved into it?"

I reply, "I noticed. What about it?"

Mom says, "It means they have met and are friends. I know Orval, the mortal crystal ruler does not want to marry yet wishes for her name to continue and be honored. That means she needs an heir who is strong. Ann is strong enough to pass as human for long times. She will need an energy to put a barrier between the mer magic and the dragon magic. Crystal magic would do that. It would also create a perfect chance for you to join them unknown. Be prepared to join them in an instant without notice. You can go play for a bit. They will be in personal space for a few hours."

I groan, "I do not want to know."

Then I go to my playroom. After a bit of playing with my toys, I go over to a corner wanting rest. I have a few blankets stacked here for such. On the way I feel something under my hand. I look. Nothing is there. I feel again and feel an elfin stone, yet I still do not see it. I hear, "Pick me up if you want. No harm do I cause. I am part of an object made from love. Do you want to know things I can teach?"

Unsure why I trust the unknown voice, I pick up the invisible elfin stone. I hold it tightly until it is no longer felt in my hand. Then I hear, "I am half the main stone off of the immortality spear. I will lead you to greatness and greatness you will receive. Your last name is hereby Peacemaker. Claim it and accept none other. You will return to the immortals having that last name and the strength it is. All you have to do is obey the commands I tell you and the laws set onto the masses by the Emperor."

I ask, "Emperor? Who is that?"

The main stone says, "He started this all. He ranks over the first ones to get magic. Over everyone they have made kings over them as well. He is the reason the magic nations exist. I will share more when you can handle it."

I ask, "You mean there is someone above Sire Kar?"

Main stone replies, "Yes."

I say, "I want to meet."

Main stone says, "You might get to one day."

Mom and dad call me, so I go rejoin them. Minutes later, we go into the immortal meeting area. Everyone is gathering. Sire Kar comes by. He stops in front of me asking, "What is your name lass?"

I reply, "I am Sam Peacemaker."

He smiles. Why should that make him smile? I run. What about the name I was given by the main stone make a king over me smile? He has never smiled to anyone or for anyone that I know of. I run to my favorite space and hide there as best as I can. I am shaking. Mom finds me hours later. Mom asks, "Are you alright, Sam?"

I shake, "Why did I get him to smile. I do not deserve it."

Mom says, "I do not know dear. Come on and join your parents as we watch the mortals again. They will need help."

I craw into my mother's arms. Soothing. I relax. Mom says, "I understand seeing sire smile scared you. It might have nothing to do with you. We do not know. Relax and learn what we can show you."

Calming I stand up and join my parents. We see the young couple join his parents, a human king named Henry and the dragon king Diana for lunch. Dragons do not have any term for queen and neither do some immortals. After they eat, Ann goes for a swim but tires before dinner. She goes back to the personal space. Mom closes the view port before saying, "Ann might be pregnant. She is acting far more dehydrated then in the week there before her marriage."

Dad says, "If she is then it is almost time for Sam to go there and learn from them. Daughter, we have decided to pass the promotion we are up for to you, but you must prove you have what it takes to get it. If you succeed, you will become an Ezzran. Failure though will make you not able to advance rank. Please do your best to help them."

I say, "I will papa. I love you both."

They tell me they love me too. Then we watch Ann and her Matt again. It is breakfast the following day there. Matt asks if Ann is still dehydrated. Ann tells him that she is slightly dehydrated. He asks, "Yet you do not drink more water?"

Ann says, "I have learned to not jump extremes. I get sick. That only dehydrates me more."

Matt says, "Alright, please hydrate enough where you do not sleep so much. It concerns me."

Ann says, "Going for a swim."

I understand Matt has no clue that is how she is hydrating her body. I also understand she has no clue he is a dragon. Matt walks with Ann to a pool room. No one else is in the room. They swim together for a bit before Matt carries Ann back to their room. Ann is nearly asleep. Once the view port closes, I ask, "Why did she not mention her magic?"

Dad says, "Fear. Some nonmagics kill magics. She must think he is nonmagic to marry him. That means she is either afraid of him killing her or of his rejecting her for how she was born."

Mom says, "I think it is rejection as they both make love movements often."

It is lunch the next day before the view port opens again. We see them eat with his parents again. This time Matt refuses to let Ann go swimming claiming it seemed to exhaust her. Within an hour she is asleep. It is three days there before Ann wakes up. I feel the change though the view port does not open and realize I have become super attuned to the couple that will teach me. Moments later, I feel Ann is embarrassed. I feel her readiness to share about her magic with him. Then her disappointment as the view port opens to view Matt alone, just outside their rooms. Mom closes the view port sighing, "Honey tell the little dragon that his sweetheart might be needing him close to her. She seemed to need him near."

Dad leaves. I ask, "How would dad know what she needs? Would not Matt question it?"

Mom says, "Your father only has to identify himself as an immortal and state that some immortals can feel other's emotions. Then state that she feels strongly of need for her husband. Matt will return to Ann."

I nod as mom has reopened the view port. We see dad do just that. Matt instantly turns around then goes back into his and Ann's rooms. The view port closes as dad returns to us. Suddenly my own weak viewport opens by the main stone. It is on a lower rank immortal. Her name is Meme. She is directly over just the mers. I hear Ann's voice say, "Meme, why would my magic flows change?"

Meme says, "Usually happens with a child. Are you pregnant?"

Ann replies, "How soon would I know for sure?"

Meme replies, "About a week along. However, outsiders do not know for four months. You could not mention it until then if you are. Also, they carry nine months so your body would have to match that for the outsiders to accept that your husband is your child's father. We know it could only be him as no one else would live, but outsiders do not know that, and you could not safely explain it to them. Are you pregnant?"

Ann says, "Bit too soon to know. Matt and I have only been married for a few days."

There is a rattling sound. Ann quickly says, "Bye Meme."

The view port closes. The courage I had felt from Ann mere moments ago is gone. She once again feels of fear. Then sadness and disappointment. Matt's feelings hit me at that moment. He is sad, disappointed and confused.

Suddenly his goes to total panic as hers relaxes. That is followed quickly by her hurt and sadness and his anger. Then comes her desire to die. I drop in pain from that. Seconds later, I feel Matt's fear of her getting hurt. I wonder what is happening. I feel Ann's going numb. Matt's concern jumps high. Then I hear Ann say, "Let go. You want me gone. I will give you that."

Matt says, "I do not want you gone, you crazy girl. I want you to think about what you do. I could have drowned. The action you did was stupid. Do you want me gone?"

Ann says, "Why are you insulting me? Let me go. Just let me die. You do not trust me; I have no reason left to live."

I do not know why I heard that conversation, but I did. Then I feel both of them hit pleasure as Ann's emotions relax. Matt soon after relaxes also. Then I hear Matt ask, "Still want to die Ann?"

Ann says, "I never did. I just did not want to live without you."

Matt asks, "So what reason do you have for trying to end my life?"

Ann says, "Matt, I just wanted you to join me. To be with me. I did not want to sound as if I was begging you to love me."

Matt says, "I prefer you to slightly beg me to be with you over scaring me that you want me dead."

Ann says, "I love you Matt. I would never intentionally do anything to hurt you. I love you and I want you."

Matt says, "I want you too. How do you feel about trying for children?"

Ann feels embarrassed as her answer is spoken. It is, "Give."

I drop asleep. Main stone chimes, "She tried to show him her magic. He was in a panic of drowning as how she did so without telling him she had something to show him. They fought from his fear. She tried to kill herself as she assumed that he did not want her anymore. They worked it out as he does want her. He wants only her. It has always been only her from the day they met. She has only wanted him from their meeting and there was no one else in her life. She barely had any friends. Sleep now child. When you wake, you can learn more."

I wake up to another gathering of the immortals. This time king Kar asks if I would sing for him. I say, "I do not think I am special enough to do so."

Main stone chimes, "Sing out the song I tell you to."

I say, "However, if Sire wants me to sing, I shall."

Then I sing out the song the main stone tells me to. It is, "Empire's song, empire's way. Long travel has gone and come again. A hard path not without its pain was chosen. I choose it again. Again, and again we have chosen this path. Long sought hard path now we find it. Traveling cross space and time. To worlds long forgot. Peacemakers to those gone before. The shards are here the shards are there, the shards will be one once more."

King Kar says, "Nice song."

I see him walk away smiling. I go to my special place and curl up into a ball again. I wonder why the empire keeps smiling at what I say. I go to sleep. I dream of someone shrouded in clouds saying, "Grandchild, why would I not want to know you?"

Not knowing any of my grandparents, I ask, "Who are you?"

The unknown voice replies, "I am the Empire."

I ask, "Kar?"

Main stone chimes, "Not him. Focus child, the voice is not his. Though he is related to you."

Then I realize that the way he said empire was entirely different then how Kar says it. I am being watched! Even now. I wake up in a start and run. I will hide. Main stone says, "As you wish. None can fine what the invisible stones hide, not even the other invisible stones of the immortality spear."

Hours later, I calm down and return to my parents seen again. Mom asks, "Where did you go Sam? We could not find you and neither could our friends."

I reply, "I took a walk to calm down. You know his smiles scare me."

Mom says, "Alright, let us not dwell on it. How about we watch your teachers again?"

I nod. Mom opens the view port as she sits beside dad. I sit on her lap. We see Ann alone in the pool room. Ann whispers, "I am pregnant. I am so very happy. I think I will surprise my Matt on his birthday in four months. Yes, that would be good."

She spoke in human language so no mers would get the message and the wateries would not share so she can surprise her husband as she wants to. Their days seem very similar to ours. Though they cannot watch others as we can. A week later, I feel Ann has a slight amount of pain, but she is not concerned about it. I do not realize I whispered that she was in pain until mom says, "I would think she is in pain. She did after all marry a dragon. All pure mers I have knowledge of had a sight amount of pain on being pregnant, however Ann is feeling it sooner than they did. She still has no clue she married a dragon. He does not realize she is a mermaid. It is almost time for you to join them. Be careful to act mortal while with the mortals."

I say, "Yes mom."

Three months later we are viewing Ann again when I see her in lots of pain. She hides it well. Matt comes near her and hugs her. She smiles at him though her pain increases. Days after that she moves away as he rounds any corner where she is. Two weeks of her completely avoiding him before he traps her in a corner asking, "Ann why do you avoid me? Do you regret marrying me? If it would make you happy, you can leave. I hope you stay though."

Her emotional pain that he would think that physically hurts me. Ann focuses on her love for him before she says, "I love you dearly and am happy to be your wife. I just don't feel very well."

Matt kisses her. Ann feels strongly of desire for a brief instant before pain drowns everything out. Matt steps back saying, "Alright Ann, get some rest and feel better soon. I love you."

Ann says, "I love you too my Matt. Just give me time to feel better."

Matt leaves. Ann seems confused yet she looks after where Matt went then very softly sighs, "I cannot hurt Matt by going there yet. Too long I would have to stay. Sleep sounds good. Matt's birthday is only fifteen days away."

She goes to their rooms. Over the next two weeks, Ann's pain increases. I see her only moving a few feet at a time before resting against a wall when she comes out of the personal space. The times she does gets less and less often. She does not come out at all on Matt's birthday. He is hurt by her not joining him and his parents for breakfast. Concerned by lunch and by dinner he is worried. Matt says, "Mom, dad, I think the doctor needs to check Ann out. She mentioned not feeling the best a couple weeks ago. She has been in tears when I go in our bedroom and curls into a ball. I was hoping she would be better by now, but she has not joined us today."

Diana says, "Alright son. We will bring the doctor to check her health tomorrow."

The next afternoon a dragon healer, who is also practiced in human medicines follows his parents and him to his quarters. As magic requires, they leave the doors open so Matt can be near Ann while the healer-doctor checks her health. Matt's parents stop at the door. Ann looks their way then says, "No Matt. I will not allow a doctor near me. She leaves or I do. I will leave and stay away for months."

Matt asks, "Ann why will you not let the doctor near you? She is here to help you."

Ann replies, "I do not trust doctors. I won't let her near me."

Feeling resigned, Matt says, "Leave doc."

The doctor leaves. Matt's parents follow. Matt sits by her asking, "Why do you not trust doctors?"

Ann says, "I do not want to talk right now."

She yawns, Matt kisses her forehead as he leaves her alone. He closes the door on his way out. Two months later, at lunch Matt sighs, "Mom, have the doc visit again. Ann is not even getting out of bed now, except to use the restroom. Whatever is making her ill has got to be figured out. Ann cares for it or not, I need to know why she is so ill."

The next day, the doctor again follows Matt into his rooms as his parents stand at the door. Ann just lies on the bed, though she feels as wanting to flee. The doctor sits by Ann. Instantly Ann says, "You may be able to check me out but you do not know my normal patterns, so I am not going to accept anything you think of as treatment for me. You are just wasting your time. It is better spent helping someone that is willing to let you."

Sighing the doctor gets up goes over to Matt and his parents as they were standing by the door and says, "As long as Ann refuses treatment, there is nothing that I or anyone else could do. I am sorry young sire. She will not let me even try to help her."

Doctor leaves. Matt's parents follow. This time they close the door. Dad closes his view port. Mom says, "Best thing she can do though she knows it not. Even if her healer were trying to help her the best thing that she could do at this point is to refuse treatment."

I ask, "Why is that?"

Mom says, "She has twins. One is a dragon. One a mermaid. Equal strength. Both are their nation's heir. If the mermaid healer helps, the dragon baby could die. If the dragon healer helps, it would kill the mermaid baby and possibility Ann. That would also kill the dragon baby at this time since she is not born yet. You will join them very soon. Remember to act as their child."

I say, "Yes mom."

Joining the Mortals

Suddenly we hear Ann calling for Orval. My view port opens to see Matt and Ann's room. Orval is just joining them. She looks around then pushes Matt away from Ann touching his shirt, while demanding to know what he did to her. Ann says, "Orval, please do not hurt my husband."

Orval looks at her entirely shocked. She faces Matt saying, "Sir, I apologize for shoving you. Please forgive me."

Facing back to Ann, Orval asks, "Friend, do you realize that your husband is a fire type magic?"

Instantaneous shock, fear, confusion and understanding registrar on Ann's face. I feel it all as well. Orval seeing the expression on Ann's face says, "You did not know."

Scared, confused and hurting, Ann asks, "Can you help me, Orval?"

Orval answers, "I don't know if I can. I will do my best however, and it could be painful, also I will have to take you away from everything you know."

Ann says, "Please try."

Matt says, "Try please, I don't want to lose my Ann."

Ann calms. Her body relaxes as Orval picks her up whispering, "Ethro follow."

The view port instantly moves to the crystal world. Mom hugs me tightly with tears in her eyes. She pauses the image then says, "Be good for them Sam. Be their daughter as much as you are ours. We love you."

Mom resumes the view port. Ann smiles saying, "Being here helps a lot and I am no longer in pain."

Orval says, "It is good you are not in pain. However, your husband would hate not seeing you for a while, you have to go back. The pain has a good chance of returning. Therefore, I am naming you my heir for your helping me when I needed it. You are now the crystal people's princess. Welcome to our world."

The heir right insignia appears on Ann then mom shoves me towards the view port. In the next instant I am in a dark place with the presence of a mermaid on one side of me a dragon female on the other side of me. They feel the same age. Very young. Between them is a crystal girl even younger than they are. The mermaid and dragon are looking at each other leery. The space is small. I realize my mother forced me to join the mortals as Merth Ann's baby. I say, "Sisters, calm down. You are not in danger from each other. I realize the space is tight, but it is only for a small while. We will stay between you two so there is no pain from the other's energy."

The three babies nod. I feel Ann searching our energy patterns, so I quickly hide all my energy signatures except mer, dragon and crystal. She will not know I am not her child. Mom asked me to treat Matt and Ann as I do them so I will. Ann is shocked that there are four of us here. She wonders how I exist. That is not something she will ever know.

Ann whispers, "One pure mermaid. Her name is Mertha, after my late grandma. One pure fire energy, I name her Diana after Matt's mother. A pure crystal magic and one that is all three."

After a slight pause, Ann asks, "Orval, do you mind if I name one of my quads after you? I was thinking Orvalina."

Orval weeps happy, "Oh the little princess has my name. I will not be forgotten."

Before she names me, I impress my name very strongly onto her mind so no other name would she try to call me. Ann says, "Not just your name. She has your looks as well. I wanted to tell my Matt first about his twins, but I was in too much pain to do so and did not want him worrying about them as well. Now I have quads. The two with crystal energy keep the mermaid and the fire energy apart. That keeps their pain down. The mermaid has my grandmother's appearance. I named her such. The fire energy looks as Matt's mother and I call her that name. The pure crystal is Orvalina. The other one has my appearance and all three magic energies. I think I will call her Sam Peacemaker. Sam as she is so strong. Peacemaker as she has peace between different magic energies. Let me surprise my Matt."

Orval laughs, "Of course. Let us get you back."

I relax as now I will have my name even when I can rejoin the immortals. However long that ends up being. Ann says, "I want to pretend to be sleeping at first. I am tired and pretending to sleep will keep them from asking me a bunch of questions delaying my rest. I will answer their questions when I wake up."

Orval says, "Alright. You should get issues sorted out with your guardians and his guardians as soon as you can though."

I know she has nothing to fear as my parents would not let anyone harm one who holds me. Ann sighs, "I know. I want my babies to live. I want my Matt to live. I want to live. If I had learned Matt was fire energy before we got married, we would not be married. If I learned before our babies, they might not exist. However, if they did happen, I would have understood the pain. I did not understand it as I did not know Matt is fire magic. Sam will know though. She will never go through pain she does not understand."

Orval says, "We leave now."

Moments later, I feel Matt and his parents near. Matt asks, "Is she alright? Were you able to help her with whatever is the cause of her illness?"

Orval says, "Relax. Ann is fine now, just sleeping. You should introduce her to your mother's people as soon as possible. It is especially important that you do."

Henry asks, "Why would that matter?"

Diana says, "If he doesn't, they might not accept her and could hurt her."

I hear a door close softly before Matt says, "It is good to see you resting peacefully sweety. I am glad she was able to help you. I hope you trust me enough to share why you were ill when you wake up."

It gets very dark here. My new sisters go to sleep. I know they are probably tired. I speed up the growth of Orvalina and myself until we match Diana's and Mertha's current age then I release the growth rate. We will be born at the same time. I refuse to wait longer or make Ann go through that pain twice. At least mommy told me childbirth could be painful and more often than not, mortals had pain. When Ann wakes up, I hear her ask softly, "Sir, how long did I sleep?"

Some male replies, "I do not know Princess, but we have not seen you for two days."

Ann thanks him then minutes later I feel Matt, Henry and Diana near. I hear dishes being set down and a soft conversation between Matt and his parents. After a bit, Matt asks, "My Ann, are you feeling better?"

Ann answers, "I am fine. Orval was right about you, wasn't she?"

I am sad as she just lost a chance at immortality from her threat against life. Matt answers, "Yes. Why does it matter?"

Ann says, "My full name is Merth-Ann."

Diana gasps, I know she understands the issue they face. I imagine she is shocked. Matt asks, "What?"

To that Diana replies, "We need to go to my parents' land now; or the protectors of the land will kill your wife."

No, they will not. They could hurt her very bad, but they cannot kill her. Their hurting her would only happen if she had intent to hurt anyone. She just honestly fell in love with a different energy type. Matt and his father ask, "Why?"

Ann states, "Because of whom I am, and that I could be a huge threat to the safety of the people. I know that I would kill anyone who was a threat to my people's safety."

Henry asks, "Who are you then Ann?"

Diana says, "It does not matter. We must go now. No guards as that will be taken as an act of war. We would all be killed. Without the guards we have a chance of living."

Ann sighs. I hear Henry say, "Kenneth, I know you are able to be trusted. I am placing you in charge for the next month while my family goes to visit Diana's people. They need to know of Matt's marriage."

The voice that told Ann she had slept two days replies, "Have a safe trip my king."

A small amount of time later, we feel too be in a carriage. Ann's breathing soon evens out. After a while, it changes. At that time, Henry asks, "Why does your full name make a difference Ann?"

Ann does not reply. In minutes, her breathing evens out again. After five rounds of this, Diana says, "We stop and wait here for a bit."

As the carriage slows, Ann wakes up. She is asleep soon though. Henry asks, "Why set up camp in the middle of the day?"

Diana says, "Just waiting for a bit."

It starts getting cool out when Ann wakes up again. Diana says, "Eat dear, we will be continuing soon."

Minutes after Ann has ate, a dragon energy comes over. He asks, "Why are you all here?"

Henry asks, "Why do you address my wife and not me?"

Dragon replies, "It is right that I should address my ruler before others."

Diana says, "Good. We continue on now."

Tired of not knowing what is going on I open my view port. Everything is slightly fuzzy, but I see Matt help Ann to her feet. I see the dragon male glance at them questioningly. We go over to a large rock. Dragon male draws the burning tree symbol on the rock then taps it four times. The passageway into the dragon land opens. Matt pulls Ann closer to his side as we go down. We enter the creator that has a desert scene above and a lush valley below us on a cave entrance where we are midway up the creator sides. The stairs we were on in the cave continue down to the lush valley. Henry asks, "Diana, why is there a desert scene above us? Why are the stairs hidden?"

Silence. Henry asks, "Stranger, would you tell me?"

Dragon says in dragonic, "My king's choice on what to share."

Henry asks, "What was that?"

Silence. Ann seems very tired. Everyone is quiet. We walk toward the only building in this creator, it is the dragon castle. On one side of the building is a small pond. On the other side is a large fire pit. It is a big area with smaller deep burn areas in it and a small fire at the center. Ann glances at the fire and her fear increases, yet she continues to move forward. The dragon stops. Diana stops and so does her family. The dragon steps to the side then backs up past Diana and Henry. He continues backing up until he is past Matt and Ann. At that point, he turns and joins the only ones that are standing. They must be the dragon council. Diana walks into the fire pit. Ann steps forward slightly. Matt holds her close whispering, "Wait."

As Diana approaches the fire, it grows bigger. I realize it does that for the royals of the nation. The dragons do the magic salute of highest respect all magics give. Highest respect ever is freedom. No magic bows and I would not accept anyone doing so to me. Diana says, "Guardians, this is my family. My husband is named Henry. You have met my son Matt. The girl he holds is named Ann. We thought that was her name for a while. She just told us it is not her full name. Turns out her full name is Merth Ann. I take it to mean that she is a mermaid."

The dragons look shocked and scared as mass confusion ensues. They all glance at Ann often while whispering, "Mermaid? Do you think she is? Why would they marry? Is she not in pain here? Perhaps Sire is mistaken about her magic abilities."

Ann leans into Matt's side. One of Meme's dragon equals commands for quiet. Not a mortal magic alive would ever disobey any immortal. There is instant quiet. Meme's equal, Dee says, "We will talk with the prince and his wife."

Matt steps forward so Ann does as well. They enter the fire pit at the same time as Diana exits the center. Diana exits the outer ring as Matt and Ann reach Dee. We are instantly in the guardian and mortal mixing area. Dee then says, "Ann, Diadon says you are a mermaid, are you?"

Without pause Ann shakes slightly as she replies, "I rule the mers. I did not know Matt was a magic at all let alone a fire type. I never mentioned my magic as I thought he was human, and it is not safe to tell humans of being magic."

Matt says, "Ann, I never mentioned my magic as I thought you were human yourself. It explains why you were afraid to hear from your friend that I am fire magic. I did not understand your fear then."

Ann instantly looks at her feet. Dee says, "So you both kept your magic secret and then got married. Tell us why you also feel as a neutral type magic to us Ann."

Understanding it is best if she holds nothing back, Ann replies, "On the way from the ocean to be Matt's wife I came across a female about my age. She was seriously hurt. I used my water magic to help her. When I became ill, I asked for her help. She came and took me to her home. She named me her heir. I gained neutral magic. It is why I can be here now. My water magic is in a low state now and it helps."

Dee blocks Matt's hearing then says, "Ann, Matt does not hear us now. Tell us are you ill for a reason, we did not attack you."

Ann replies, "Yes. I am with children. I feel four. One for each nation and one that has all three magic types. They are draining my energy. The fire was hurting me until I gained the neutral magic. Until I did, I only had twins. I have not told Matt yet as he was worried about me with my being in pain. I figure the mer girl and the fire girl felt threatened by each other. The other two calmed them down. I will tell Matt soon if we live."

Dee asks, "You think we would kill you?"

Ann replies, "In protecting your people you would be in the right."

She is not that big of a threat even if I was not here. Dee says, "Protecting the people would be right, but you are not a threat to them. It is clear you love Matt more than anything, except the babies. Yes, we will allow you to surprise him. The dragon child is able to rule here and so is the one with all three energies. Pure dragon will rule here. The three-magic child will have authority over her, but I think it would hurt her mer abilities to stay here. She should stay with you."

I am pleased she thinks so as mom and dad chose Ann and Matt as my teachers. I wonder what they can teach me that my parents cannot. Before anything else is said we are back in the dragon nation's fire pit. Dee releases Matt's hearing before saying, "We accept this union."

Excited Matt says, "Accepted."

Matt spins Ann slightly before hugging her slightly tight and kissing her. Ann feels to enjoy it, but I notice my new sisters needing air. Ann apparently notices as well for she pushes Matt back saying, "Matt please. Our babies need air."

Matt is surprised. Then excited he asks, "Babies, as in more than one?"

Ann replies, "As in quads. There are four."

Matt looks Ann over then asks, "How far along are you?"

Ann laughs as she replies, "I became pregnant the night we were married. Mers do not show until they are starting the ninth month along. The babies are why I am so tired all the time. I was in pain as one is a complete dragon and one is a complete mer. They were scared of each other. The other two calmed them down."

Matt questions, "When were you going to tell me?"

Ann says, "Originally I was planning on your birthday, but I slept clear through it. Then you were worried about my health and I did not want to increase your worry, so I decided to wait until I was not stressing you. After that I was not sure if any of us would live so I waited. Now we only have to talk to my guardians."

Matt becomes sad. He says, "They could end my life."

Not any more than your direct guardians could kill Ann. Ann shakes her head, saying, "No Matt, they cannot. I would protect you. I would hurt for a while if we lose our babies, but I would die if anything happened to you. I just need to tell them what happened since I left the mer nation. Our babies are innocents. They will not be harmed."

Taking Matt's hand, Ann leads him over to the pond knowing her guardians would know it as soon as she touches the water. She holds Matt's hand with her one that is mer marked. That mer mark is so small only immortals can actually read it. Still holding Matt's hand, Ann use that hand to touch the water as she says in mer royal language, "Mer guardians I know you are strong enough to know what I say. I am safe. I am in a fire magic land as my husband is fire magic, a dragon. The guardians here have accepted our union. I am with child. More than one. I feel different as I gained crystal magic, it is a neutral type. Do you accept our union?"

They better not reject the union. My parents accepted it. The pond ripples then mer words appear. The words read as, "Crazy child for marrying a fire magic. However, there is no retraction of our acceptance of your marriage, glad you are and will be safe. Come to the nation before your children are born."

In magic common Ann says, "Thank you guardians."

Ann faces Matt saying, "They accept us. I just have to go to the mer nation before our children are born. Chances are they will be born there. That is not something we have say in. My people do not know they exist. The crystals do as Orval told them. The dragons just heard it, but my people do not know. It will be difficult to adjust to pressure differences while pregnant. Once they are born, I could make the trip easier. Remember I saw you every other day while we were just starting our friendship. I made the trip upriver in two hours to the point you led me through the forest to. Downstream to the ocean's depths took me an hour. My culture revolves around sea life because I am a part of the sea life."

Matt laughs. Then asks, "Mom says that she originally thought of having you wear a high slit or low V-neck dress, but you refused. Any reason for that?"

Ann replies, "My mer marking. I have one that covers my upper chest, wraps around my body and ends on my thigh. I did not want anyone seeing it. Besides that, only you get right to see my body."

Matt says, "Funny, but I never saw the mark."

Ann says, "I had my guardians suppress it, until after I had told you about my being a mer. I had worked up the courage to show you then we had argued. I guess you did not realize I could keep you safe. I can breathe air and water. I breathe out air when I breathe in water. I was intending to help you and show you where I am from. I am too far along in my pregnancy to do that now. Maybe later. I cannot even change into a mer yet because as soon as I do my nation's calling will get strong enough to take me back there until they are born."

Matt understands. While they were talking Diana tells Henry about them going to the guardian space, that everyone listened to the woman as she had learned how to live forever and achieved it. Diana tells him that she had explained to everyone who Ann was, and that the flame grows for the royals of the nation. She also mentions she was not sure how to mention this place as many have attacked her people, the desert scene helps her people stay safe, that everyone stills when an immortal talks so to hear and follow any instructions in hope of learning how to live forever, and that the language was her native language; the language of this place.

At that moment, a dragon flies in and becomes a young girl. Henry looks ready to attack the child. Diana moves between them just as fast as mortals can process the intent to harm. I understand Henry has no idea he married any dragon let alone their ruler. Diana says, "You do not want to try to harm anyone here, I will protect my people."

Henry asks, "What do you mean?"

Diana replies, "I am a dragon, their king, we have no word for queen, and our son is a dragon too. We will protect the dragons from any threat."

Main stone chimes, "Dragon ways are why some immortals do not speak of queens. They speak of kings and spouses. They started as dragons. You will be a king. For the mixed started here. Do not accept anything less."

Henry asks, "*Merth-Ann* is she a dragon too?"

Diana replies, "Not a dragon; a mermaid. If she had been a dragon it would not have been necessary to bring her to meet everyone."

That is right. They would have known her. Ann would have had to pass the council's test to marry the nation's heir. It is that way in any magic nation. Ann says, "Queen; I am the queen of the Mers, not just a mermaid."

Diana says, "That explains how come you are strong enough to survive."

I am sure the nobles would have begged for help long before Ann did, and the commoners would not have been able to handle it. Diana tells Henry all magic common laws and further explains why she does not talk about this place. After he understands it all, we go back to his nation.

Learning

We had been gone a week. On getting back, Kenneth submits to Henry and gives his report of a boring week before asking how the trip was. Henry says, "It was good. Diana's people are happy for Matt and Ann."

Soon after Henry writes magic common laws into the laws of his nation. Wow! That will make things easier for me. Thank you, grandpa. That evening, when Matt and Ann are in their quarters, Matt asks, "Can I see you as a mer?"

Ann asks, "Do I get to see you as a dragon?"

Matt replies, "Sure."

He shows her his dragon looks. Pure bright purple scales larger than a mers. His wings are silver. Ann whispers, "Yum."

Matt changes back saying, "Mom and I are the only purple dragons. Her color is darker than mine. I am nearly certain our dragon baby is a shade of purple also."

Ann says, "Mer royals are purple as well. Crystal royals are purple tented white. Yes, all four have a shade of purple for their aura."

Matt questions, "Mermaid?"

They move into the bathroom. Ann fills the tub with water then fully dressed climbs into it and relaxes. Mertha changes to her mer appearance as Ann does. Mer scales come out from our waist over our clothes and then forms our tails. Ann says, "Maybe later we could go swimming alone in the ocean Matt. Just the two of us. Well from here anyways. We could come across some wateries or some mers. Especially if I show you where I grew up."

Matt says, "Sounds good. Would I get to meet your parents?"

Changing back to human appearance and getting out of the tub, Ann replies, "Sure."

Mertha sighs and changes back as well. Matt says, "You are extremely attractive to me. Both ways. I drew your image the day we met, even without knowing your name. I wanted you even then. I regretted not asking you for your name when I did not figure ever seeing you again."

Ann says, "I wanted you that long too. You are so yum to me. I mean everything about you appeals to me. Even your dragon looks now that I have seen them. The guardians were my first actual friends, they treated me without the respect my people did. Martha was my first mortal friend. Her extreme need for help made me respond when I hid from most until I could learn about them. She helped me learn about the human's language, that is common here and what different terms mean. She helped me learn what is able to be eaten. Things such as yeast, she could not explain what are and I avoid them because I do not know. She joined the mer nation so she could live there easier. After she did that, our friendship was strained as I was in authority over her. You were my next actual friend. Your helping me when I was so in need made a lasting impact in my mind. I have a few friends now. None know I am a mer. They do not even know I am a royal. In the first few weeks after you helped me, I referred to you as Mr. Yum. Say something!"

Instead of saying anything, Matt kisses her. Ann responds by wrapping her arms around him. Then Matt asks, "Still want me to talk?"

Ann mutters, "What do we need to talk about? Yummy. I am glad you love me."

Matt says, "I am the lucky one. I got you, fish girl."

Ann giggles, "That is fish queen. I rule after all. You just call me love, Ann or beautiful. Then again I do not mind you calling me my fish."

Matt laughs. Ann leans against Matt. In moments, her breathing evens out. Matt carries her to their bed. I close my view port. Main stone says, "You know to obey your parents and treat them as your parents asked you to, you will have to call them mom and dad not Ann and Matt."

Having not thought of that, I sigh. Thinking it over, I realize the main stone is right. They will be my mortal parents so I will have to call them such. A month later at dinner, Ann says, "It is time I go see how my people are doing. I need to ensure their safety. Are you fine with my going there?"

Grandpa, grandma and Matt nod. Matt says, "Let me walk with you to the river please. At least I can see you off safely."

Ann says, "Sure. I would enjoy your company Matt. If anyone asks where I went, mention I went to see my parents and catch up on events."

Matt walks Ann to the river before telling her to be safe and make sure their babies were safe also. Ann says, "Of course Matt, see you as soon as I can. I will get a shell etching done of them after their birth so you can have it."

As if anyone could sketch one that is not their own magic. My siblings are not even strong enough to sketch themselves. Matt says, "Sounds good. The sea awaits. Come home soon."

Ann looks around making sure they are alone then walks into the river. She lowers herself to the water height and swims downstream as a human. By the time she reaches the ocean twenty minutes later, she is exhausted. Ann says, "Wela, please help me get to my nation."

A young water royal comes over to Ann asking, "What is wrong Ann? I have seen you swim that distance many times easily, yet now you tire?"

Ann replies, "As if you do not know. I am pregnant. Please help me."

Wela asks, "Are you having a son or a daughter?"

Ann states, "Daughters."

Wela gasps, "You pluralized it. Twins."

Well as all mortal magics have only had only two babies at the max and most of those are singles, I understand how she would automatically assume that. Ann states, "No. Quads. I am having four."

Wela wonders, "You are joking right?"

Ann yawns. Wela asks, "Can I stay for their birth?"

Sleepily, Ann mutters, "Um hum."

Wela holds Ann as she moves down. Seconds later, Ann says, "There please for a moment."

I open my view port wondering where and why. We go into a cave. A water force dragon of low ranks is there. Fishes! We are in danger! The water force is not to be messed with. The water dragon shoots a water ball at us. Thankfully, Wela steps in front of Ann and absorbs it. Only a water could stand up to a direct hit of the water force warning ball. Meme shows up and calms the water dragon down before saying, "Dangerous to come here with your babies Ann. I am sure you understand the reason that is."

Oh blast! I did not know Meme was in the water force. Ann replies, "Diana and Sam."

Meme says, "The one yes. The other is a mer. Not sure which one is which."

Ann says, "I just wanted to thank the guardians again for accepting my union to my Matt. I could not live without him anymore. I could not. We argued once. I nearly killed myself from that. It was when I was going to tell him about my being a mer. I scared him. He reacted in that fear. We argued and I tried to kill myself. He prevented my urchin from doing as I had ordered it to dry me out completely then he assured me he loved me and explained I had made him think I was trying to end his life. He understands now I was going to show him the mer nation."

Meme says, "Go there. They need to know you are pregnant. By the way, you are starting to show."

Ann says, "Oh, beautiful… Wela, please."

We leave the cave. I relax as the water dragon does not follow us. I try contacting my parents to let them know what I just learned, but I am not able to. Must be water force interference. At least I assume so. I wonder why one is so close to the mer nation and why Meme acts as a low rank guardian. Wela helps Ann to the mer city. In moments, the mer healer clan leader is near us asking, "What happened?"

Grinning Wela says, "Look closer healer. Your queen is pregnant."

Mer healer looks again then smiles, "Of course! What is the baby's name?"

Ann says, "My parents should have been at my wedding. They would have enjoyed meeting my husband and his parents. I am glad they accept my union to him and accept him into their family. I wonder…."

Healer says, "Pardon Queen, but wonder what?"

Ann does not answer that either saying, "Library first Janice. I need the ruler's staff."

We go to the library then to the throne room. There Ann calls for a national meeting. In minutes, every mer is in their normal seats here. It is quiet as they all wait for her to talk. Ann says, "Martha, thank you for helping me know how to behave and talk on the land so I could pass as one of them. As everyone knows, I left here to get married to one I love and live with him. His name is Matt. That was eight months ago. I return a bit earlier then I had expected to as I am eight months pregnant."

She pauses to let that sink in. The mers all say, "Congratulations on your baby."

Ann shakes her head saying, "Not baby. Babies. I am having quads. Four daughters."

Everyone has extreme shock at that. Ann continues, "I named the pure mer maiden Mertha after my grandmother. After she is three days old, she becomes your queen, so you all do not have to worry if your queen is safe. Martha can raise her with help from my parents, the council and the guardians. Know that once she is five, she will come visit her family where I live now for a few days every year. She will be here most of the time, but I need to see her too. I think her being your queen is best for all of us. I do wish to bring my Matt here and let him learn about how I grew up. On the way to become Matt's wife I help the queen of the crystals. She named me her heir. When she died, I became their queen as well. It is fitting then that the pure crystal girl is named after her. I call that baby Orvalina. My friend was named Orval. Something that she said before taking me to meet her people explained the massive pain I was in at the time. She was right. My Matt is fire energy. He is the dragon prince."

Mass confusion and fear run around. The volume level jumps from silent to everyone talking at once. Ann commands, "Calm down!"

Instant quiet though I doubt any are calm by any means. Ann continues, "I had the same reaction you all just did. Mine was worse as I was concerned for my life, my babies' lives, and Matt's life. The guardians of all nations involved accept our union. I named the pure dragon girl after Matt's mother Diana. She has her looks as well, except my eye color instead of the red color Matt's mother has. She will one day be king of the dragons as they have no word for queen."

As Ann pauses, someone asks, "What about your fourth baby?"

Ann replies, "Her name is Sam Peacemaker. Sam has all three energies, my appearance and right to rule over all her siblings. She cannot live in any of the magic nations she inherited skills off of or lose skills from the others. Therefore, she has to live with Matt and me in the human nation. Yes, I understand the dangers that causes for her, but I am sure she will be able to pass off being human to the humans. After all Matt and I both thought each other was human. We would not have gotten married if we suspected otherwise. I wanted to let you all know before their birth. I also promised my Matt he would get an etching of the four of them together. Orvalina and Diana will be placed in their magic nations after I leave here. I am very tired now, good night."

Yawning Ann walks out. A young mer woman, the healer clan leader and Ann's parents are quick to follow her. The young mermaid woman asks, "Why do you honor me so?"

Reaching the library, Ann leaves the staff there with the other ruling items. Ann replies, "You are my friend. One of the very few I have. The guardians, the council, you, Matt, and a few others are all that treat me as friends. The guardians I show the same respect to that my people show to me. Even if they do not enjoy it, I do not know how else to act. The council talks to me about things in the nation but as their clan's leader it is partly their job to do so, to ensure their clan has needs and issues taken care of. You are the first one that treated me as a friend."

She is Martha then. Martha says, "You saved my life. I was a stranger and you saved my life."

Ann replies, "Your information has saved me many times. It continues to serve me and help me remain hidden among the humans. I just saw Matt looking as a dragon a month before I came here. That is when he saw me as a mer. Mom, were you excited to have me?"

Grandma mer replies, "Yes. When I told your father, I was expecting to have his baby, I thought he could have jumped clear out of the ocean in one leap. It only added to my happiness."

Ann laughs, "Matt seemed grounded which was the calm I needed after the stress of needing the approval of his guardians and mine. I was nearly sure Meme and her equals would not retract their acceptance of a union and I am glad they did not, still I had to ask. It was the guardians Matt falls under that I was stressed the most about. I mean I had unknowingly joined their people and I am not even that energy type. I was a threat and I knew it. They accepted us. Then I knew I was safe, so I told Matt about our babies. I had planned on doing so earlier, but I slept through his birthday and then he was stressed because I was in pain and tired a lot and he did not know the reason. I did not want to add to that stress. I knew the tiredness was expected but the pain I had was far greater than anything recorded in the archives. I could not figure out why so much pain. I figured the mers before me had downplayed the pain so others would not avoid having babies. I realize now they did not. Of course, fire and water babies in a confined space would feel threatened by each other. Orvalina and Sam stay between Mertha and Diana. The pain now is at the level I read about."

Breathing heavy, Ann leans against a wall for a few moments. From my view port I see her have her eyes nearly shut. Healer says, "Get some rest Queen, your mother and I can get you to your room."

Ann says, "I am sure you both could. I just want to walk there on my own if I can."

Grandpa mer says, "Do not over do yourself Ann. Pregnancy certainly took a lot from your mother and she only had you."

Ann says, "I am sure. However, I am still alert and intend to walk."

Five minutes later, we approach the ruler's quarters. Ann appears drowsy. We enter a sitting area. Ann stretches out on a couch made from dead coral. As I notice her asleep, I decide to show her my appearances and items. Ranking above Meme's boss, (at least the one who would be if she were not in the water force) Zeffron, I am able to use that one's items. I activate the time spear. Ann and I are six years in her future now. She is in the forest above the dragon creator. I see her there as I fly over. My rainbow-colored appearance attracts her curiosity. She follows me. I jump our location to the crystal world. When she moves toward my crystal home, I jump locations again putting us in the great room here. Ann is sitting with Matt, Mertha and my mer grandparents. I am on the throne as Mertha had gave it to me as soon as I approached her. That means all mers here will accept my authority over them. I go for a swim. Ann understands that I am the reason she sees these things as she notices my tail is the colors of a rainbow. Getting very tired as I am not used to taking others through time, I end the use of that, making sure to put us back in Ann's proper time. I activate Zeffron's energy spear so she can wake up and for energy myself.

Ann wakes up then seems confused. I am sure she is trying to sort out what I put her through. Healer asks, "How do you feel?"

To that, Ann questions, "Why are you asking?"

Healer says, "You were asleep three weeks. How do you feel?"

Ann says, "It was so real."

Healer asks, "Queen?"

Ann replies, "My dream. It was so real."

Meme commands, "Out! I will talk alone with Ann."

Meme and Ann are left alone. Meme sits by Ann. Instantly Ann tries to show her respect by trying to sit up. Meme places her hand on Ann's chest saying, "Relax. That was not just a dream Ann. Sam is rainbow-colored. You saw future events. At least boss said you had activated his time spear and the images you saw were shown. We all want to know how you did it. It is entirely under boss's control, yet you managed to use it. How did you do so?"

Ann states, "I am not even sure what you talk about. Sam seems to be different though. As if nothing is wrong. As if her sisters were not drained. As if I was not tired. Why is she so alert when none of her siblings or I have energy?"

Main stone chimes, "Be more careful child. I will tell you what to say to deflect their wondering about you now. You cannot be using their items without hiding that fact. Until we get you to learn how, you should not do so."

Zeffron shows up saying, "Interesting. My energy spear lit up and it is focused here. Yet you have no extra energy. Are you sure it is Sam?"

Ann says, "What are you talking about? Sam is more alert then I am. That is all I am sure of."

Zeffron asks, "Sam are you using my spears?"

Main stone tells me to say, "How would I know how to? Am I that special?"

I do that. Ann looks confused. Meme says, "Ann when a magic is not born but is asked a question, their mother answers what they would have. It is the mother's voice to the child's words. Do you understand?"

Ann replies, "I expect as much as any could without being an immortal."

Zeffron asks, "Sam, did you use my things? Yes or no."

As the main stone tells me to, I reply, "Ask your boss's child if you can find that one."

I am the child of Zeffron's boss up some ranks. Anyways, I think that will at least divert his attention from me. Main stone was right, I need to be a lot more careful when using immortal items until I am back with them. Zeffron and Meme leave. Ann goes to sleep. I relax. I wonder what the main stone can teach me now. Main stone says, "Very well, I will teach you mer traits first as you are in the mer nation."

In hours, I have a far greater mastery of my mer abilities then I ever thought possible. Then I go to sleep. I wake up a bit later and the main stone teaches me a far greater mastery of the crystal abilities then I ever thought possible. I finish that and go to sleep. When I wake up again Ann is waking up also. I open my view port. It is slightly clearer than it used to be. The mer healer clan leader says, "Queen, you were asleep five days. How are you feeling?"

Ann says, "Let us go to the throne room then so anyone can see my babies as soon as they are born."

Grandma mer and healer help Ann up. They go to the gathering room, where the throne is. Someone sees them head there, so in minutes all mers are gathered. I close my view port knowing they would fear seeing it, fear me, fear what I might be able to do. Plus, I do not need the questions and the attention it would cause. Minutes later, Diana pulses a slight red then is not with us. I hear the mers mutter, "Cutie for a dragon."

Then Orvalina pulses white. She is no longer with us. The mers mutter, "A sweetheart."

Mertha pulses blue. I am alone. The mers say, "Beautiful."

The three colors pulse over me and I am with everyone. Silence greets me. I look around and everyone has their heads dropped. I see some trying to sketch into different coral sheets. I figure they are trying to etch my image or even my sisters' images. After a few minutes one shows Ann what was etched. Ann says, "Sorry, not even Mertha seems right."

Ann looks at every etching the mers tried to do of the four of us young but mentions only a few could get Mertha's image correct and none got anyone else to look or feel the way they should. My turn. I shift my appearance to seven then say, "Mom, they cannot draw people they do not know the symbols of. Let me. I will show you my symbol."

Seeming shocked at my appearance change, Ann nods. I take a blank coral sheet and etch in Mertha fully. Then show it to Ann. She mentions it looks almost alive. I smile and show everyone else. Many mers comment on the strong resemblance. Turning the coral sheet back to me, I etch Orvalina a bit away from the etching of Mertha. I show it to Ann then everyone else. They comment the same way. I face the coral sheet to me again then form a triangle with the images, I etch in Diana. I follow that up by etching their symbols on the inside of that I draw the symbols together in a circle and a triangle. As I do so, I say, "I am Sam Peacemaker. This is my symbol and my looks."

My image etches into the center of the image by my magic. Only I can draw that. I hand it to Ann saying, "A gift for my parents."

Ann looks at it then says, "Thank you Sam. It looks so real."

I say, "It fades. The image needs traced by the one of each nation that raises my sisters. You chose Martha to raise Mertha. She should trace the etching with a scale from Mertha. That will make it last."

Surprises

Ann gets a scale off of Mertha, hand it to Martha with the etchings and has her trace the etching of her princess. She does so then places Mertha's scale back on her. Mertha touches her smiling. Ann, Mertha, Healer and grandma carry us to Ann's rooms. We get some rest. I hear the nation celebrating the birth of quads, two of which are mer royals and soon to be queens. I say, "One queen! One king! I never drop rank from the dragon normal. I am after all part dragon."

Their calls change from 'long lives for our soon to be queens' to 'long lives for our soon to be king and queen, sisters born.'

That I accept. The calls last the rest of the day. Wateries join everyone the next day asking to meet the mer quads in the royal line. Ann allows them. I move away from all of them. No one will pick me up except Ann or Grandma Mer. Ann was the one who carried me to her room. If it had not been her or grandma Mer, I would have stayed in the throne room all night. The wateries and Waters leave just before dinner. Diana seems really weak and tired. I realize she is hurting here, especially after so many watery and mer females touched her. I change my appearance to seven again then pick my sister up. I extend a crystal field around us, completely blocking everyone out before I use the dragon breath to heat up the inside of the crystal barrier. Diana relaxes as it gets warmer. I stop when her health gets normal. Then I go to sleep releasing my crystal field. At least Diana will live now.

Three days later, Ann calls a national mer meeting. In minutes everyone is gathered in the throne room. There Ann turns over the rule to Mertha giving her the mer ruler's ring. She hands me the mer ruler's bracelet showing I have more authority then Mertha does. Again, calls for us to have long lives rise. The mers sing, "Long lives to King Sam and Queen Mertha."

Ann puts Diana, Orvalina, and me into a carrier and leaves the mer boundaries before saying, "Ethro follow."

We are now on the crystal world. Ann looks over everyone then goes over to a strong couple that is not part of the council and says, "Madam, please use a bit of her crystal to trace the etching I had done of her so it will last. I am asking you and your husband raise her with help from the council and the guardians. Orvalina will come visit her family once a year where I live once she turns five."

They say, "We are not worthy to raise our young queen. Why us?"

Ann says, "You are strong and kind. She needs that. Could have been anyone. You are the first couple I saw with strength outside of the council. I am sure they will help you teach her to be good for the nation. The guardians also. I need to go take the little dragon to her home now. Bye. I might not be back."

The woman says, "You honor us."

Then she takes a bit of sister's crystal and traces the etching I had done. When she finishes, she places Orvalina's crystal back on her. Then Ann places the crystal ruler's ring on Orvalina and gives me the matching bracelet. That is also more authority here then Orvalina has. From there Ann travels directly to the dragon nation. The dragon's glance at her nervously. Ann says, "I just bring my dragon babies here."

Dee says, "Bring Sam and Diana Diadon here."

Ann obeys asking, "What does that mean?"

Dee says, "Diadon is the last name of the dragon ruler. We call the nation's heir Día. Sam is over Diana but Diana rules here. Only the council as a whole could raise Diana for you. Anything you want to say before you leave with Sam?"

Ann replies, "Diadon Diana will visit her sisters in the land that I now live when she is five and older once a year. I do not think I will come here. I do request that someone that will help raise Diana use one of her scales to trace an etching I had done of her so Matt can see how his daughters look. It is starting to fade, and I was told that doing as I asked would make it last."

Dee does that then rejoins Diana's scale to her body. Handing the coral sheet back to Ann, Dee says, "Please leave and do not come back without Diana or Sam inviting you. The dragons are leery of your being here."

Ann says, "I understand. Thank you."

Then Ann climbs the steps followed by the warrior clan leader and his wife. We leave the dragon home and head towards ours. Though Ann could travel faster using crystal magic, she chooses to walk. I realize she has a bit to think over and adjust to. As Ann walks carrying me, she whispers, "It is extremely dangerous for a magic to live with humans. Especially one so different than any one magic. It just has to be. I must make sure she has a good chance at life. How to do that I need to figure out. Also, will others accept her name?"

Near sunrise, we enter the forest that surrounds the city she now calls home. A few moments later, we are surrounded by the pick of the hunters from the tiger pack, with the pack leader. I smell them before Ann notices she is surrounded. Ann is nervous. Yet for some reason she sits down slowly. Ann holds me out slightly as one sniffs the air. Ann says, "This is Sam. She is Matt's and my daughter."

The pack leader is closest to us. I put off a very small amount of fairy magic so it will know we are friends. It licks my arm. I giggle as it tickles. Ann relaxes slightly as I do not mind the tiger so close. The tigers walk off. Ann stands up, hides me again and walks into the nation's capital that is home now. Ann goes to the castle nodding to whoever speaks to her. Mostly they say, "Princess, Sire Matt will be glad you are back."

As I am hidden under a cloak no one realizes my existence yet. Ann goes directly to Matt's and her quarters. These will be my rooms until rooms are chosen for me. I see Matt's whole expression lights up on seeing Ann. Ann smiles at that before rocking side to side. I giggle enjoying swinging. Matt beams, "Is that our youth?"

Laughing, Ann closes the door before replying, "This is Sam. She is our daughter, it is dangerous for her because of her heritage. She needs to be allowed to fight, so she can protect herself without showing any of her magic."

Then Ann hands him the etchings and says, "Sam did it. Someone from each nation traced the etchings to make them last. Told you their names already. I had them a month after I left. That was a few days ago. Let us take care of Sam."

Matt says, "Come on."

He leads Ann to his parents' quarters. There he requests the four of them talk alone. They invite us in. Grandpa closes the doors behind us, before asking, "Talk about what?"

Matt says, "Ann had our daughters. As she mentioned in the dragon nation, only one is with us. Ann named that one Sam Peacemaker. We hope the people accept her name as it is. Also, she needs to be allowed to fight, so she can protect herself without using magic. If she is not allowed to fight, some could put her in a tank to stare at her mer form, take from her crystals that are part of her life or kill her because she is a dragon. The people accept Ann fighting as they know she was raised in a place that allowed and encouraged females to fight as well as the males. Unless females are allowed to fight here, Sam would be shunned for learning it and the warriors would not allow her onto the training fields. I do not want her to have to sneak around to learn things to stay safe."

Henry says, "You have some good points. Can we see our granddaughter?"

Ann says, "Do not touch her. Magic makes her skin lethal toxic to most males. Only the one she marries would not die from touching her."

Then Ann moves the cloak. Grandpa says, "Got your hair color and face structure Ann."

Ann replies, "Has Matt's eyes. Our other three will visit once they turn five. The dragon girl I named after you Diana, as she has your appearance. She rules there now. The crystal girl is named after my late friend Orval. Her name is Orvalina. She rules the crystal people. Orvalina looks almost as Orval did. The crystal magic made a very strong impact on her. The mermaid girl I named after my late grandmother, Mertha. She looks as images I saw of my grandmother. Grandma ruled before papa. Papa passed rule to me when I announced I was engaged. Now Mertha rules. Sam cannot stay in any magic land without losing skills from the others, so though she is magic she must live with us. I am glad to have her here, but I am scared for her."

Grandma asks, "Can I hold Sam?"

Ann looks at me, leaving the choice up to me. I stare back forcing her to decide. After a minute Ann says, "I have no idea if she will let you, but I am fine with that."

As Ann places me into grandma's arms, I go to sleep. The energy I took from Zeffron's energy spear has finally wore off. Main stone says, "Now that you have been near dragons, we can advance your skills in those traits. Focus on your dragon fire child. What color do you see?"

I reply, "Dragon fire is red of course."

Main stone asks, "Is it? Is everyone's dragon fire red? Are you sure?"

I ask, "You mean some are not red? What color are they?"

Main stone says, "Your dragon fire since you picked me up is not pure red as low level dragons are. Focus on it and tell me what colors you see."

I do as told to. I whisper, "Red, orange, yellow, white, green, purple, and blue? I suppose that comes from being mermaid mixed."

Main stone says, "No child, it does not. Blue fire is the hottest fire there is. Red is the coolest fire. Most dragons are in the red to red-orange flames. A few are orange to yellow. Less than that are the yellow to white flames. Green is the healing force of the immortal dragons; ones that are only allowed to do healing. Purple are any that are able to get into the upper ranks of the immortals. Blue fire can only be achieved by a slim number of people. You have the ability deep in you to bring it out, just as you have the ability to learn red water and clear life. The three skills are all buried deep in you. The hotter your base fire becomes, the easier you will be able to use blue fire when you are ready to. Wake up!"

I wake up in grandma's arms. Without meaning to I breathe out a small fire. Grandma smiles before saying, "Trying to show off for me young one? Let us see your dragon looks then."

She releases me into air. I drop two inches before I change. Grandma startles back shaking. Dad trembles. Oh blast. They are scared of me. Why are they afraid? Main stone chimes, "Dee is multicolored."

I change back to human appearances taking appearance of five. I say, "Grandma, dad, I look so strange as the magic mixed in me. All my magic appearances are strange. Did I startle you?"

Grandma says, "I only ever saw guardian look that way before. I was frightened."

Dad says, "Same here."

I say, "Maybe they were magic mixed before they got guardian rank. Only they could say for sure. I know grandma and dad can teach me dragon things. Mom can teach me mer things. Grandpa can teach me how I am to behave near humans. Hum, someone needs help. Crystal knowledge in the open fields, show me what is not known to many."

Saving another

They look confused. I see a small girl run into a crystal mine in another nation. She tries to hide in the caves. Some older male is chasing her. I do not care for the look on his face. Ann says what I had but drops in pain. I say, "Mom, you must increase your base energy before trying to do that. It is a hidden secret in the royal ranks. I learned it when my base energy increased. Please relax and let me focus on the one needing help."

After they nod, I say, "Crystal magic can take on different appearances. Do not make noise or touch my gem as I help the child until I return here and tell you so. Touching the gem or making noise would put me in danger. Start now."

They nod. I take out a small rainbow crystal and say, "Open doorway to the child in need of help."

The crystal expands to be the size of a child's door. We all see the child running from the man. My mortal family all look protective of the child in seconds though she is a stranger to them. I make my appearance change to a creature of dirt, rocks and lava. That ought to scare the man well enough to leave. I instantly step through the gem doorway. I end up between them. They both startle as I stepped out of the gem. Facing the man, I hiss. He backs up. I make hunger motions looking at him. He flees fast. The child says, "Please do not hurt me. Please. I will not tell anyone about you."

I drop the strange looks then face her. I ask, "What are you talking about child? I am here to help you. That was just a disguise. Effective, well designed and useful to protect myself and others. Are you alright?"

The girl stutters, "Yes… I think so. Who or what are you?"

I say, "Neither matter. Go home."

The girl says, "I…I cannot."

I ask, "Why not?"

The girl says, "He is our next-door neighbor. I only just realized how yuck he is. He ran from you, but he will share of how he saw you. The hunger movements you made. He would not run again if I am safe and the town would hunt you. He is trusted in the town. My parents will believe I am dead. After all, a creature that looks at an adult as if it would eat that one, could surely eat a child."

Main stone chimes, "Ask her if her parents trust her. Ask if they have any gems or glass in their home."

I ask, "Would your parents trust you that such a creature is safe for you to be around?"

The girl says, "If they did not think they see a ghost. That could only happen if I managed to get home before he got to the town. He has a big lead."

I say, "Not necessarily a problem. Do your parents own any gems?"

The girl says, "We are poor miss."

I ask, "How about any glass?"

She replies, "A small glass mirror. Why do you ask?"

I say, "How do you think I got here? I moved through the gems. Glass is slightly more resistant to traveling but not impossible. Where is the glass kept in your home?"

She says, "Bathroom."

I say, "That is a problem. Personal private space I cannot even look into. Those who have magic respect those spaces. Only your extreme need near something I can see through got me to look in on you today. If I sent you into your town, could you get to your family before he does?"

She replies, "I would try to."

I say, "Alright. How long did you run before reaching this cave?"

She says, "The sun was high overhead. I am not expected back until dinner."

I check the sun's position in the sky to see that it is about one hour after high phase. Then I feel the movements in the surrounding area for any towns in that traveling distance for a young child. Only one town. I say, "I found your hometown, I think. I am going to open windows to every public space there. Do not talk while they are open. People would hear you. If you touch one, you travel to where it is viewing. Be careful. Immediately go home and move your glass into a public space. I will talk with your parents."

The girl opens her mouth to say something. I quickly cover it. I shake my head then write on a paper, "Remember not to talk."

After a moment she nods. Then she looks over all the scenes I have open. At one she looks concerned. Another she looks at sadly. Then another she points to. I close all the view ports before I ask about the three. She says, "Papa was in the one, he was hurt. Mama was in the other, her tears made me sad. The one I pointed to is someplace I recognize."

I say, "I could take you to your mother as she was alone. Willing to trust me?"

She replies, "Yes miss. I am Lilly. What is your name?"

I reply, "I do not speak my name without issuing commands over others. I have no desire to command you what to do."

Lilly replies, "O…k."

I reopen the viewport that she looked sad on. I say, "Miss, why do you cry?"

The woman jumps then looks around before nervously asking, "Who is there?"

I reply, "A friend. I know your daughter Lilly. She sought me out when she needed help a little bit ago. Why do you cry?"

The woman says, "Lilly is dead. She was killed by a monster."

Lilly says, "No mama, I was not. My friend is good with her disguises. She protected me by looking as a strange creature. I am by her now. How can I prove to you that I am safe?"

Her mother says, "Why do you and your friend not show yourselves if you are my Lilly?"

Lilly looks at me. I take her hand saying, "You want us to show ourselves? Fine then."

With that, I step through the glass, pulling Lilly through. I say, "Madam, I am Lilly's friend. I took a disguise of a strange creature to help her. The bad part of that is now people will look for such a creature. I would appreciate it if you do not mention meeting me. You see Lilly is safe."

She asks, "How can I be sure she is not someone else in disguise using a voice recording?"

Lilly says, "Scarlet."

It must be a code word in their family because the woman quivers, "My Lilly, what happened that you needed that help?"

Lilly replies, "He tried to get me into a bedroom alone. I ran. My friend helped me. I assume he is spreading lies about my having been killed."

Her mother says, "Yes. I am not even sure if I am still sane."

I say, "You are. Convince your husband to leave this town. Go to the gem cave to the west. I will give you instructions there on where to go to stay safe and your family can live together as you should and want to. Lilly must go with me back to the gem cave as he reached this town before she did. Any family you have and trusts you can come there safely. We must go now, someone approaches, and we cannot be seen in the town by many if your family is to stay safe."

Slow what you show others

The woman nods. I take Lilly back to the cave, tell her to wait there for her family then as night came on, they were to head west with only those there at that time. I say, "Take them to the nation that nears the sea. I will have a home made for your family by the time you get there. If you need help call out for it. The magics hear those calls even if we do not watch others. I do not watch many without cause."

Lilly says, "Thank you for helping me."

I say, "See you when you get to my hometown. It is the capital of the nation."

Then I step through a gem and travel back to Henry, Diana, Matt and Ann. I close that gem then say, "You do not mind building their family a home, do you grandpa?"

Henry replies, "Let me know how big it needs to be to suit them. That one male was disturbing. He better not try anything with any of my citizens, not even the newest ones."

I yawn then say, "That took more energy then I thought it would. I want to learn fighting as soon as people would accept my doing so grandpa. I do not want to face males that are that ugh without being able to defend myself."

Henry says, "Agreed. You learn fighting as soon as humans would accept that you can. I see magics advance faster than humans, a lot faster. You need to act more along our normal though. You can be a bit faster, but not as fast as you showed me today."

I ask, "How fast can I be?"

Henry says, "You could be a few weeks to a couple months faster then normal and it would not be questioned. Can you read?"

I say, "Most things in the languages I know. If I cannot, I would ask one of the four of you."

Henry says, "In the library is a book about child growth. It has an image of a baby on the cover. Read that to learn how most babies behave and act as they do. You can be a bit faster on learning things but looking as a six to eight-year-old days after your birth is not safe."

I nod, yawn then look as a baby again. Henry asks, "So mers can change their looks easily Ann?"

Ann replies, "No. Crystals can but I am not skilled enough to do so."

Henry says, "I will call for a national meeting tomorrow. It is late. See you in the morning."

Matt and Ann go back to their quarters with Ann carrying me under the cloak again. I get some rest. An hour later, is normal breakfast time. All of my mortal family meets for breakfast in the throne room as usual. No one realizes that we had very little sleep as they took energy drinks. I smell it from Henry also, so I know Diana convinced him to drink something he has no clue what is made of. Henry dings a bell then tells the guard that steps in that his advisors were to be here in an hour at most. The advisors arrive in half an hour. Henry says, "Call a national meeting. Immediately. I have some announcements to make."

Kenneth replies, "Aye Sire."

Two hours later, we go to a town square where many people are gathered, including all advisors. Henry says, "Thank you all for coming and showing my family respect. Matt and Ann have had children. Four daughters. Ann left one in the nation she is from as that one is the future ruler of that nation. One she took to a friend's nation as Ann was the named replacement for their ruler who had no child. So, one of the quads became the heir for that nation. One she placed with Diana's people as their heir to the nation. The fourth one is my heir. I am here by declaring that either gender can fight. I will not have people trying to hurt my granddaughter because of her gender and that she will one day rule. It would be unfair to allow her to learn fighting and not others therefore all people can learn to fight. Also, I am decreeing that the names Sam and Samantha are reserved for the royal family as Ann named her daughter that is my heir Sam. No arguing about her name. I know it is male version but that will keep her safer. As will her being called king after I die. Ann, please let the people meet Sam Peacemaker. It is now the nation's name.

That officially makes it her last name. Sam can rule upon her eighteenth birthday or if I die and she is at least eight. She was born five days ago."

In moments many come forward requesting to change their names. All that do so were called Sam or Samantha. My sisters in that instant call out that Sam and Samantha were honored royal names reserved for their king Sam and her descendants. Their people in moments have removed the name from their lands. It is now only my name in the entire nation I have authority over. I am pleased my sisters respect me so much and surprised the humans respect Henry enough to do so. Ann hides her surprise well. Diana and Matt are used to the respect he gets so they are calm.

After that is all done, Henry says, "A seamstress sewed a flag with the symbols Sam wears from the nations Sam has heritage in. Please lower the Monax flag and raise our new flag, This is the Peacemaker's nation. Long live the people."

The people call back, "Long live the Peacemakers!"

King Kar joins us laughing. I shake. Ann steps back. Kar says, "No need to fear me young one. It has been a long time since I saw anyone gain so much respect so quickly. I know what caused it. You are not sure, are you?"

Ann asks, "Sir, who are you? What are you talking about?"

Why would a King...

Kar says, "Sam knows why she fears me. Yet somehow even a water force respects her last name. Why do they fear a child more then they do one who is a king?"

Main stone chimes, "Submit to a king over you."

I see Kar's eyes widen in shock then he says, "Sire who are you? Might I know your name?"

Humans and magics ask, "Who is he talking to?"

I do not wish to answer him. I do not deserve his respect and I am unsure of him calling me a king over him. He is over me. Why should I get his respect so? I should have to answer him, but I do not. The main stone chimes, "I am Peacemaker of course. My first name is not your concern at this time. Even among so many I could hide. One day you will know who I am. How are your children?"

Kar leaves. A magic person asks, "Who was the empire talking to with respect?"

Ann says, "I wonder why Sam was afraid of him. Are you sure he is the empire?"

The fairy that happens to live in this land says, "By sure. I was once in a flower field when someone I respect was talking with guardian rank. He came by. The guardian called him the empire. It took me weeks to adjust."

Ann trembles. I think I need help. Main stone asks, "Who do you want here Sam?"

I think my mom would be best. Main stone chimes, "No, you cannot have her here. You look similar to her. That connection cannot be known yet. I think I will make this decision for you."

In the next instant, Ancient Poem is walking over to us. She looks confused then walks closer still. She asks, "What are your daughters names miss?"

Ann replies, "Mertha stayed in the land I grew up in. Orvalina stayed in the land a friend had passed to me. Diana, named after Matt's mother, stayed with the people that are part of her past. This little one is Sam Peacemaker. She is heir to this nation."

Poem says, "She has that name? The last name. No wonder people respect her. That last name always has commanded respect. It always will. People with since do not anger one with that last name. Pure uncontrolled energy. Even so, those with that name can control the energy they have at a far greater level then even those first to use the energy. Why did you give her that last name?"

Ann replies, "Could not think of any other name for her."

Poem steps closer then as she looks at me, she trembles. Ann asks, "Miss, what is wrong?"

At that poem looks at her saying, "A future in which the spells can see, why would a king submit to thee? Why does the king let you hold her? Why does she hide even now? How soon will she join us in the Ancient ring of the empire?"

Main stone says, "Ancient! If a king over you wishes to be unknown, you should let that one be unknown. We train Zeffron to get a promotion. That is not something we can do with the immortals."

Poem looks down saying, "No one but my king and I remember my being here or our conversation. King Sam, the memory mix will be very effective. I look forward to seeing you in the empire's capital."

She leaves. I look around and see the memory mix go over everyone around me. No one remembers her being here, or what she said, not even Ann. I am shocked that the first poem called me a king over her and so did Kar. Why would I rule over them? Main stone asks, "Are you afraid of me child?"

I do not think so. I have no reason to be. Main stone chimes, "No reason to fear me, yet you do. You fear what I can teach you. You fear other's responses to you. You fear becoming a king of the spear empire. Even so you held me close. You chose me after I came near you. Still afraid would you still choose to pick me up?"

Scared, I wonder what else I can learn and if it will help me get over my fear. Main stone says, "Help you get over your fear? Child there is no getting over fear. You just learn how to ignore it until you are no longer afraid. Library as soon as you can. We got to know how to act here."

I agree. After the people all get to look at me, it is lunchtime. My mortal family eats alone. As we eat, I whisper, "Mom, library after lunch, please. I really need to read the book grandpa mentioned."

Ann says, "Matt, would you show me the library after lunch. I crave information. It is what brought me to this city, and to you."

Matt replies, "Sure sweety."

After lunch they take me to the library. We are alone so I shift age to seven. Ann hands me the cloak she wore last night and this morning saying, "In case anyone comes in."

I thank her and put it on. No since in taking unnecessary risks. I start at the young books. By dinner I have read half the books in the library. I change back to baby looks then we go to dinner. That night, while Matt and Ann are asleep, I sneak out of their quarters and go to the library under the cloak Ann uses. I avoid the guards as I can feel them before they notice me. I seal the room then read every book I did not have time for earlier. It is sunrise when I finish. Main stone chimes, "Zeyla could visit you there at that time. Only if you let her though."

Of course, I would let my real mom visit me. Seeing her would make me happy. Main stone says, "Sure then. Right now, you need to get back. Ann would panic if you vanish and the people would question your being here without them at this time."

I hurry back to Ann and Matt, going to sleep in the crib they have for me as a baby, the cloak in a bundle nearby. Ann wakes me up ten minutes later. Being an immortal, I can adjust to little sleep far easier than they could have so I am alert in a few moments. We go to breakfast. I start on slowly showing a month-old baby movements, letting the humans see them. One comments, "Young princess is very advanced."

Ann smiles, "Where I grew up, that would be average speeds. A sheltered city that not many born outside of it could be allowed access. The warriors there attack first and ask questions later. If you made it to the city, their warnings would be hard to forget."

Matt asks, "If I were to go there?"

Ann says, "You are not fool enough to try without me. They would not attack any member of the ruling family."

The human asks, "What nation are you from Princess?"

Ann says, "A sea going nation. I have no desire to tell you exactly what nation that is."

Katana

The day goes by fairly relaxed. At night I once again sneak to the library. There, the main stone contacts my mother, Zeyla. In minutes she has joined me. I hug her tightly. Mom asks, "Adjusting to mortal limits Sam?"

I reply, "Mostly. I miss you and papa."

Mom says, "I know. We miss you too. We cannot come here often without giving away your identity to the mortals. That would make you fail your test. I do however have a gift for you."

I ask, "What is it?"

Mom shows me a sword. Then puts it up and hands me it in its carrying case. Mom says, "Do not use it. The katana is only held by immortals. This sword belongs in our family line. My mother gave it to me. She got it from her father. It is now yours. Your using it would instantly tell others where you are. A failure of your test. It has two effects. The effects are done by how it is used, the intent behind the one using it. The effects it has are one causing an easy acceptance of others' genetics even for immortals. A baby would result from the two that touched in a few hours of the effect being used. By such you were born. Your father and I really wanted you, so we asked a boss to do so for us. Neither effect can be done to yourself, or for yourself. If you use that effect on someone, you cannot mix your genetics with theirs. The baby would be mortal with a short lifespan. Such as days, if even that. The second effect it has is banishment from immortality, removal of all magic and the one who was banished could die within fifteen years. Only a traitor to empire ways should ever be put through that. I hope you never have to do so. Anyways Sam, Zeffron's boss was told that his boss's child holds the katana. Zeffron knows his direct boss does not have a child. Your using the katana for any reason will instantly tell them who you are. I need to go now so you stay hidden. Ancient Poem only granted me so much time hidden from everyone. Do not call for me again. If you need help, I will send it to you. I watch over you. Love you Sam."

I hug her tightly for a few moments as I tell her I love her to. Once I release her, she leaves. The katana is left with me. I hide the sword under a floorboard as it is too big for me to carry around until I can walk where others accept it, then I go back to Ann and Matt. I again make myself look as a baby and fall asleep in the crib they have for me. Ann wakes me up a few hours later. I am sad as what mom told me felt as a goodbye. Main stone says, "I thought seeing your mother would make you happy."

Depressed, I think, I was happy to see her, yet her words seemed to be a goodbye. Why did she tell me goodbye? Main stone chimes, "It is not forever. After all, you are both immortals. You will see her in time."

Sighing I check on Lily and her family to know how big grandpa will need to build the home and how soon they will get here. It is just her, her parents and one other female, I am guessing is a younger sister. They are about a three-month journey away. I go back to Matt and Ann's quarters because I will not get my own until I am five.

Ten minutes of sleep before I hear my mortal parents waking up. I stand. Ann gives me a disapproving look when she comes into the living section of the rooms. I whisper, "Checked on Lily and her family. It is her, her parents and a younger girl I think is a sister. They are three months away. Grandpa needs to know."

Ann nods whispering, "Back to baby looks."

I obey. At breakfast, Ann in magic common tells grandma what I had said. Grandma then leans close to Henry and tells him what was said. Grandpa nods. After the meal grandpa asks his family to walk together. We walk the town, me carried by Ann. The first place big enough to build a house is near the town square. I have a special purpose for that area so use mer language to say, "Somewhere else."

Most would assume I did baby cooing. Ann looks at me then asks, "What other spaces are there for what we all agreed to?"

A home for a family

The next space is uneven. It would take to long to level it enough while keeping it safe to build a home before they arrive. I again use mer language to let Ann know. Ann says, "Sir Henry, would it not take a bit to get it safely leveled? We do need it in a time frame before the group arrive."

We move on. The next one we come to is decent. I silently ask the main stone what its opinion is. It says, "A home could be built here without too much difficulty. It does not matter to me except you made the promise they would have a home when they arrive. Keep the design simple to save on production time. Simple and basic furniture and let them personalize it to their tastes. I say a four bedroom so guests can stay the night if they want or they could use the space as an office or storage room. Time you should try rolling over. Remember to act as if you struggle a few times before actually doing so."

I mutter in mer, "Four bedrooms."

Ann says, "I think four bedrooms would suit the family that we expect to be joining this nation. At least the messages we got seem to suggest such."

Henry says, "Agreed. Is this the site we agree on for the home?"

Ann says, "I think so."

Matt says, "Looks fine to me."

Grandma says, "Sure. They will be close enough we can see if they need help adjusting to this nation's ways without traveling a way."

Grandpa says, "Let us go back to the castle and design a place for them."

My family goes to the castle. We are alone, so I shift age appearance to seven and sit by them. I whisper, "Four bedrooms so they can have guests stay over, use the extra as an office or storage space. I am thinking a simple structure. Decent kitchen and two bathrooms, simple beds, dressers, small mirrors, some bedding, some dishes and a couple outfits to get them started. Nothing fancy. Let them personalize their space. We can get them the outfits after they get here."

Grandma sketches out a few floor plans. Then we decide on one. Grandpa says, "Construction will start tomorrow then."

I whisper, "Guard approaching."

With that, I change back to looking as a baby. Ann sets me on the floor. I pretend to play with my hands. There is a knock then on command a guard enters. He says, "Pardon Sire, I was hoping to have my vacation earlier then usual this year. My cousin is getting married and I was hoping to be there as we are close. We grew up together. Could that be arranged?"

Grandpa says, "Go enjoy the event. Family is important. I expect you to check in when you get back is all. When will you leave?"

Fooling others on my strength

The guard replies, "One-week sire. Thank you."

I pretend to try to roll over onto my gut. The guard says, "Princess is getting strong."

Grandpa says, "We see that. Anything else you need?"

Guard replies, "No sire. Thank you again for your generosity."

He leaves. Then the staff deliver lunch. I again act as if I try to flip over. One of the maids says, "Come on Princess, you can do it. You are so strong and smart."

She has no idea exactly how strong and smart I am or that I consider it easy to flip over. I smile at her to thank her for what she assumes is a compliment. Then I try again to please her, just because I am needing to advance my growth appearance again, so everyone accepts it. I act is if I almost get it. She gives me some more encouragement. All the servers are staring at me now. I decide it is good and flip over. The servants erupt into applause. Grandpa says, "Good job Sam. Everyone needs to get back to their jobs now."

They take the dismissal as an order and leave my family alone. Grandma softly says, "Keeping up as fast as you can get away with, I see."

I change back to looking seven and whisper, "Of course. I am tired of being carried everywhere when I can walk as it is. I will not make them question it though, so I put up with the being carried. I intend to advance as fast as I can get away with."

The next day work starts on the new home. I keep up advances in movement as fast as I can get away with. Three months later, the home is completed. The next day, Lily's family comes in. Grandpa says, "Welcome. We have been expecting you. A child told us she had used a disguise to save a girl from an older up to no good. One of the girls with you is the description of the child that was saved. The home just got finished yesterday.

We left it basic so you can personalize it. There are four bedrooms and two bathrooms. The extra bedroom you could use for guests, an office, storage or if you expand your family. We got some bedding in your new home and some dishes to get you started here."

Grandma asks, "Do you all need any clothes? We are willing to get you a few outfits each to help you out after your emergency move."

Lily's mother says, "A child about Lily's age saved her. I take it that child works for you. Where is she? We want to thank her. Thank you for the offer, but we shoved all our clothes into bags and have what we need. We could use some food to last a bit and jobs if that is not too much to ask."

Dad says, "Food. We should have expected you would need some. Well, this way makes sure you will actually use what we buy for you."

Mom says, "That is right. Anyways, it is good you all arrived safely. Though I am sure your daughter's friend would make sure of that."

My family laughs. Lily says, "Where is she? I want to thank her."

Grandma says, "Around someplace. Let us get your family some food and show you to the home we built for you."

We do that. After we do mom, and grandma help them carry the food into their home. Mom whispers, "Your friend got your message Lilly. She is far better at disguises then you realize."

In mer I say, "Mom, they need to know who I am, so they do not put me in danger later."

Ann looks at me then says, "Diana, please have our help leave us alone with this family. We need to talk to them alone. That informant is unknown, and they must know to not hurt her later."

Grandma says, "You are right. They know enough to be a threat to her and not even know it. They must know. Leave us! If my husband asks the reason you did tell him Enno and that I will explain later."

The guards leave. Ann hands me to Grandma. Then she puts up a crystal shield around the house before saying, "Alright, we are safe."

Grandma releases me. Lily and her family startle. I instantly change to look how Lily met me. I say, "Surprise Lily."

Lily asks, "Who or what are you?"

I say, "I am a magic and the girl who saved you. I am months old here and most do not know I am a magic. It must be kept that way. You know my older looks so I had to let you know who I am now to keep safe later. None of you are in any danger here. Do you accept that Lily?"

Lily says, "Thank you for helping me escape him. My family should not move the mirrors out of the personal spaces. Our new princess can see through them anywhere else."

I say, "I could but mostly do not. Some things that get me to are extreme need or my name. I will not tell you what it is because my doing so is issuing commands over anyone I tell my name to. Can we trust you all not to put my life in danger?"

They all agree. Lily asks, "Are all the royals here magic? How about the people? What magic are you?"

Grandma says, "My husband is not magic but accepts all of us. He is the only royal of this nation without magic. There is a mix of magic and nonmagics in the nation. I am a dragon, so is my son and two of my four grandchildren. Ann married my son. She was born a mermaid and was given crystal magic. Her four children are one of each magic and one that has all three magic and photographic memory. The three you do not know you will meet when they are older and able to defend themselves."

At that I laugh, "Grandma, they already can. They just wait for the time mom set. Do you think they dare disobey the commands she issued in doing so?"

Grandma says, "No. Back to baby looks. We cannot stay long here without guards. After all, this family just moved here. We should be concerned about them still. At least that is what many would expect."

I nod obeying. Ann picks me up and we leave. Back at the castle, alone for lunch grandpa asks, "Why did you send the guards out to us Diana?"

Grandma says, "The girl and her mother have met Sam. They needed to know so they do not react to her in shock later when she is older and then have to explain the shock. This way they have time to adjust to it without putting Sam in any danger."

Grandpa accepts it. More time passes by as I fool the staff into thinking I improve on my skills faster than most children my age. I move everything at a month or two faster than human normal. The people think I am a strong genius. Months after I turn one, a foreign king comes in while my family is eating dinner. He asks for a treaty. I make the mer then dragon noises for reject. Ann and Matt look at me. Grandma says, "Henry, have I taught you what that second sound means in my native language?"

To that Grandpa says, "Remind me."

Grandma says, "How about Ann tells us the meaning of the first sound Sam did, as I am sure she knows it."

Mom says, "I think Sam let us both know the same thing. At least I am assuming they mean the same. Do they, Sam?"

I nod. Grandma says, "Henry, Sam highly objects to a treaty with him. I am not sure why, but she did both Ann's and my native languages for reject."

Grandpa asks, "Why Sam?"

I say, "Lento nation is his ally. Given the treaty the Lento nation wants, why should we consider his?"

Grandpa says, "Sam, we should hear him out before making such a decision. To do so before hearing him out is unfair and biased. To be a good ruler one must be fair, unbiased, and willing to make decisions individually."

Ally?

I say, "That is true. It is also true that allies stay together. He is allies with King Lento who hates the magics and they are our allies. Do you think the magics would not take it as a threat to their safety?"

Grandpa says, "My granddaughter has some good points. What exactly are your treaty terms?"

The visiting king asks, "How did she learn I have a treaty with Benjamin Lento before even meeting me?"

Grandpa says, "My granddaughter's informant team is very skilled."

He asks, "How old is she?"

Grandma says, "Old enough to understand. How does her age affect any treaty?"

He says, "It does not. I was just wondering as she sounds twenty but looks maybe two."

Then he goes on to state his treaty terms. When he finishes, I use magic common to say, "My opinion has not changed."

Dad says, "Agreed."

Mom says, "Same."

Grandma says, "Henry, none of us want the treaty he suggested. Ruler of strong allies is here."

Grandpa says, "All of my family rejects the treaty. I side with them. Thank you for visiting. Please leave."

As he does, Zeffron walks in. Grandma, dad and mom stand. Remembering my parents' command to act mortal along with the main stone's saying that my failure would get it to leave me, I stand as well. I cannot let him know yet that I outrank him. Besides, I do not need to make my teachers fear me. Zeffron asks, "Sam, how did you know about my boss's child?"

I do not know how to answer that. Main stone chimes, "Tell him it was a guess."

Without pause, I say, "I guessed."

Zeffron says, "I doubt that."

Main stone chimes, "Ancient, your king needs your help here now!"

Ancient Poem helps

Ancient Poem walks in. Zeffron instantly drops his head. Poem says, "Remember what I told you. Anytime you need it, go ahead and do so."

Zeffron asks, "What is that?"

I question, "Is that a promise Ancient?"

Poem says, "I pledge my help when you need it. Leave Zeffron."

He obeys. Poem leaves as well. I look around and see the memory mix effect everyone. I figure none of them remember Zeffron was even here. I certainly am not going to ask. Main stone says, "Ancient and the kings are the only ones that can use the memory mix more then three times. Careful doing so."

I silently agree. It is not long before I fool the staff into thinking I learn many things far faster than most babies do. I often hear them commenting that one might think I was a year older than I am. They do not know I am near when they say it. One of my favorite activities becomes scaring the staff. However, after a few times they complain to grandpa and he reprimands me for it. I accept his words and have him call an all staff meeting where I publicly apologize for scaring them all. They assure me it is alright, but I reply, "No, it is not. I deliberately did such knowing you would not care for it. That is wrong. Forgive me."

They do. I almost have free reign of the castle and grounds. The only places I cannot go without my parents are the armory, kitchen and tool shed. Those are because of my age only. One day I wonder into the throne room and no one is there. I know I will rule one day so I go sit on the throne, just to get used to the idea. After a bit, I get bored and flip upside down, so I am looking up. I think of my real parents as I do wondering how they are doing and when I will see them again. My superior senses let me know people are approaching, but I know only the castle staff and my family can move unobstructed through the castle so there is no reason to be concerned.

Minutes later, my family come in. I flip off the throne and salute willingly releasing the throne to grandpa as he is the ruler here. Grandpa says, "Sam, others will not respect you if they see you sitting so."

I say, "No one will. If the guards knock when there are strangers around, no one will see me sitting so. That is no one who does not already respect me."

Grandpa says, "Time for you to explore the town. You need to introduce yourself to the people."

Traitors

I say, "They all know who I am. Why should I introduce myself? How would I?"

Grandma says, "Introducing yourself to them lets them know you care about them. It also gives you a chance to learn at least some of their names and the town layout. It lets you learn the normal of the town atmosphere, so you know better when things seem off."

I say, "Very well, as you suggest."

Then I go into the town with my parents. Guards follow a few feet behind us to protect us if we have need, mainly me as I am heir. I do not need it, no one here hates me, I can feel it, plus I can move faster than they can. However, I let them do their jobs and as I have not been trained on the defense and use of weapons, I should not show them that I know well all of that. I see the people bow, but I reject their doing so. I know only humans would. The magics hide behind the nonmagics so the nonmagics do not realize they do not bow; they salute or just nod at us.

I see one girl so absorbed in her book she does not see us or hear anyone. I go sit by her saying, "Hi, what is your name?"

She replies, "I am Jane, who are you?"

Not once has she looked at me. I say, "Sam."

Instantaneously, she jumps to her feet and bows. I am hurt by her doing so and in magic common say, "No, no I do not want slaves, do not do so. Please do not do so. I do not accept it now as you don't understand."

Then I run off. I cannot handle the first one I decided to talk to doing so. However, I want to know what occurs, so I turn invisible in an alley and go back. I hear Matt say, "Sam does not want anyone to bow to her. You will lose your freedom if you do. It is a law she follows from one of the other nations she has heritage in. Sam shows respect by touching the hand she uses the most to her opposite shoulder as a salute. If you trust her, do the salute. If you do not trust her, just nod. I think she had enough of all the bowing today and I am sure she rejected it as you did not know."

I go into an alley, turn visible and walk out to them. I say, "That is right papa. I follow all laws of the nations I have heritage in."

Jane faces me and salutes. Pleased she is willing to adjust so easily I smile and nod at her. Then I see everyone salute me or nod. My smile gets bigger as I now know none of them will become slaves. Mom says, "Well Sam, do you want to eat lunch in town, or in our home?"

I ask, "Can we try some foods in the town? Might some guests join us?"

Mom wonders, "How many guests?"

I say, "Lily, Jane and their families. Can they join us? I want some friends."

Mom says, "It is alright with us dear. I do not know if they would be comfortable with us though."

I say, "Perhaps not. I can ask though."

Facing Jane, I ask, "Would you and your family be comfortable joining my family for lunch?"

Jane says, "We have plans for today Princess. Perhaps some other time."

I say, "Alright."

Mom says, "Go ask Lily and her family if they want to join us."

I do so. They also refuse claiming to be busy. I then tell my parents I am not hungry and go to the pool room. The guards question it. I just snap, "I can swim! I swim better than mom and she swims better than dad. Ask them if you do not believe me."

They let me swim though they do not leave the pool room. What I told the guards is true for both sets of parents I have. I have doubts that both Jane and Lily told me the truth. I do not know why they would see fit to lie to me. They could tell me the truth and I would not force them to join us. I refuse to ever ask them again. I have no friends. I swim hard for hours, getting out just before dinner. At dinner mom asks, "How was your swim Sam?"

I sigh, "Fine. Why did Jane and Lily give excuses?"

Mom says, "We are royals Sam. They might not want to be around royals unprepared for any questions that come up. It is a normal thing. Plus, Lily might be uncomfortable with your heritage. It does make people leery."

I sigh, "I wish they would have just told me. I will never ask anyone again. I am alone and only I have my name so on my saying it, I am instantly known. No friends. Just lessons. I am going to go draw."

My mortal family nods. I walk out. Main stone says, "Draw later. Right now, I have something to show you. Cave tower to the top we go."

Not sure why it wants there but I go to the cave tower. I enter at the bottom, to fool the guards then change and fly up. I think the highest cave would do. However, the main stone says, "No Sam, we go to the peak."

I obey. As I reach the top, the chime that lets dragons know a human is entering goes off. I turn invisible. Moments later, two of the male castle staff come in. One says, "I overheard sire muttering in his sleep. He said dragons in cave tower. Personally, I agree with the King Lento from years ago that they should all be destroyed. However, I respect King Henry. Most things I have no issues with. That though is bothersome. We should not ally with those beasts. I cannot believe his family did not remind him of all they are said to do. I hope Princess does not learn to trust those beasts."

The other male asks, "What do you intend to do if she does trust them?"

First male says, "After King Henry dies, we eliminate the issue."

Second male asks, "How?"

First male says, "Getting rid of the royal family is the only way. Permanently."

Second male says, "There has to be another way."

First male says, "It is us or those vile beasts at this point."

I am getting angry. Main stone chimes, "Sam! If you hurt anyone in anger, you lose me."

Sadness. I silently wonder, "What am I to do about them planning on killing my family because of the allies we will always have?"

Main stone says, "Easy. Tell Ann what you overheard. Let the mortals deal with the mortal issues before it comes to the point that they think it will."

I ask, "Is that what you wanted to show me?"

Main stone says, "Why would you need to be up here then? Think child! I had no clue about that. We wait until they leave."

Five minutes later, they leave. In those five minutes I heard enough of their plan to kill Matt, Ann, grandma and me after grandpa dies to make sure they are convicted of treason. As soon as the door closes, main stone says, "In my space only I exist. Time and place no longer matter as events past are seen present."

I feel my whole-body quake then I see the Ancients shatter a spear. I see the biggest stone on the stunning spear break in half while all the rest of the stones break into three or more. I see the man I had dreamed of shrouded in clouds pick up half of the big stone. I see me pick up the other half. Yet my elfin stone is so small it fits in my hand at five? My body quakes again, then I am back here in the cave tower. Main stone says, "I have other things to show you and teach you, but you are not ready for it. Go let Ann know what you overheard."

So, I fly down, change to human appearance, turn visible and go find Ann. My mortal family is just finishing desert. I go touch Ann saying, "Mom, can we talk?"

Ann replies, "Anytime dear."

In mer I say, "I cannot decide how to punish traitors. Grandpa should. I overheard two talking about killing all of us for the treaty with dragons."

Mom asks, "Why not let your grandma know directly, or all of us?"

I say, "To dangerous for me to do so."

Ann says, "Alright. Diana, our Sam overheard some traitors planning to kill us for the treaty with strong allies."

Grandma asks, "Could you point them out?"

I say, "I do not have to. Reso has them and will bring them shortly."

Two minutes later, Reso and two males come in. One of the traitors asks, "Sire, had us summoned?"

Reso nods behind them. Grandpa says, "What are the charges you bring against them Reso."

Blocking the door, Reso says, "Sir Monax, I accuse these two of plotting to kill your family after you die for your treaty with the dragons. Watery."

I say, "I second the motion. I was in the room as they plotted to kill us, even me because we are friends with dragons. Long live the empire and its people!"

Grandma, mom, dad, Reso and a few others repeat, "Long live the empire and its people!"

Grandpa says, "Two voted against you. To the dungeons with them. Let them live to see Sam become king after me."

I say, "I have no desire to change that sentence. I despise your plotting to kill any who have not harmed you."

The first one to speak in the cave tower says, "I hope you are hurt by one of those vile creatures you trust so much."

I laugh, "You think I have reason to fear them? You fool, they call me king. I rule them! The treaty with dragons will never be revoked in any place I have authority over."

Grandma says, "Sam! Others do not need to know."

I say, "Nothing they can do about it. The ruler of the dragons called me king giving me authority over all of them. I have no reason to fear the dragons. Fools that threaten my safety or life though do."

The traitors are taken away. I know the guards wonder why I sit upside down on the throne, but they do not outright ask, so I pretend I do not know they wonder about it. Anytime grandpa comes in when I am sitting that way, I instantly flip off the throne, and stand beside it saluting him. The guards have taken to knocking before they enter at all. Most of them have no idea that I know if strangers are around even if they do not knock.

⸺ ⟿⟀⟀⟀⟀⟿ ⸺

Unicorns and fighting lessons

In the next few years, I make direct pathways to each magic nation, though only letting others know of the pathways for the magic they know I have. I also make hidden rooms in the castle. I hide these rooms from the humans, so only the magics know they exist, unless a door is left open. One such room is a magic library. I put it right beside the library everyone knows of. In it, is a vast assortment of magic books and knowledge along with the important documents of the nation, such as birth certificates, death certificates, wedding certificates, and treaties. All magic items or items that referenced magic are locked, only one that has the symbol that is on them can read them. The records must be kept safe from humans since we have to be concerned about traitors.

Today is my fifth birthday here. My sisters have come to visit. After they are introduced to the people, they all face me and publicly call me their king. Then we go into lunch. As we eat, Zeffron comes in. My mortal family and I stand. Grandpa was the last to do so. Zeffron says in magic common, "I have a couple unicorns for you Sam. They only let their owner ride them or tell them what to do. The permission can be given to others by the owner and ownership transfers in the bloodline unless the owner gives them to someone else. Unicorns choose who they belong to and both of the unicorns I brought today have chosen you as their owner. They can talk and all royals in three generations understand them. Everyone else though seems to only hear snorting. They gather excess magic to help their owner. I do not know much about them. The items you need to care for them are on them."

Gasping, my sisters go crazy with their praise on my managing to get such rare, beautiful creatures let alone two of them. I simply say, "Sisters, calm down. Let us go see the gifts."

My mortal family and I follow Zeffron outside to the castle grounds. Two horses come over to me. I realize in that instant they are the unicorns and their horns and wings are hidden. I touch both of them saying, "Male is Pegasus. Female is Una. As I am female, I will ride Una more. I will make sure I give Pegasus attention too. Teach me about them please."

Main stone chimes, "I can tell you more about them then he can. I will wait until he leaves."

Zeffron teaches me as much as he can over the next hour then leaves. Grandpa had thanked him for being kind to me then asked why he did not get my sisters anything as we were all born on the same day. Zeffron replied, "I left gifts for them in their hometowns. Only they can open those gifts."

My sisters instantly thanked him saying, "You honor us."

After Zeffron leaves, grandpa says, "Time to learn how to fight young ladies. I will not have any of you hurt and not able to at least attempt to defend yourselves."

My sisters laugh, "Grandpa, we have been taught to fight. Our lessons started two years ago."

I sigh, "I had to wait until today. Never take it easy on me sisters. I must learn."

They agree. We go to the warrior training fields. The warriors have all gathered. Grandma having assured grandpa that the dragons would protect us today. My sister Diana had agreed. Grandpa says, "Warriors are to teach my granddaughters all they can. Diana, you start as you were named after my wife. I know why that is. You look so similar to her."

Diana says, "Thank you grandpa. It is an honor to be compared to grandma. My people speak highly of her."

In ten minutes, she has completed the course grandpa set up. Mertha is next. She completes the course at eleven minutes. Orvalina is next. Her time is nine minutes. Then is my turn. Main stone chimes, "No magic, no guidance. You will master this on your own."

I struggle with the course. I fall often, get lost a couple of times and ache much when I finish the course at forty minutes. Grandpa says, "Your mom seems to think you are the strongest of the quads, Sam. To me it looks as if you are the weakest."

Diana asks, "Sister did not do as we did?"

I say, "My life is in more danger than yours is. I must be able to handle more."

Diana says, "Sisters, we were in the wrong. We used our better senses, yet our king did not. We should redo it without the advantage."

I say, "No Diana, make things as hard as you can on me. It is better for me in the long run. Grandpa is right, I am weak. I have not been able to be trained until now while the three of you have had two years under intense training. Let us just move into the next exercise."

Diana asks, "You sure?"

I say, "We need to know how advanced I must get. Make it hard on me."

My sisters reply, "As Sire wishes."

The rest of the day is spent on defense lessons. I can barely move at the end of the day. My sisters help me inside for dinner. Ann gasps, "What happened Sam?"

I say, "I am just sore. Relax mom. My sisters would not hurt me."

Ann says, "I did not think they would. The guards might."

I say, "Their Princess? Hardly. That is their mistake. They will learn soon enough not to go easy on me."

Mom sighs, "I do not want you hurt Sam."

I say, "Better to be hurt in training then in combat."

Mom says, "I know. It still hurts to see you in pain."

I say, "Let us eat."

Instant healing/ speed learning

After dinner, my sisters help me to my quarters. They offer to heal me, but I refuse them. Sighing, they leave me at the door to my rooms. I slowly move to my bed and lay down. At that moment the main stone chimes, "I help you now. Rainbow recovery."

Instantly I feel as I did this morning minus the birthday excitement. I go to sleep. I dream of repeating today's training many times. Healing many times. Until my speed is at my sister's times. I wake up fully sure how to do the exercises I went through yesterday. My sisters meet me at the door in the morning and are instantly surprised I am not still sore. I say, "Relax. I recover fast. Let us go to breakfast."

My parents and grandparents are also surprised at my recovery. I just say, "I heal fast. What are we training on today?"

Grandpa says, "Reviewing yesterday's lesson. You struggled far to much, especially as your mom insists you are the strongest of her quads and they did around a fourth of your time."

I say, "Alright."

We eat then again go to the training fields. I am told to redo the course. Today, I finish at eight minutes. Grandpa says, "You were not trying yesterday."

I say, "I did my best, but I was slow. I thought of it for a bit last night while my body recovered and woke up certain on how to do it."

Grandpa then has me move on to the defense training. I ask the guards to do their best against me. The first one moves slow and even a human could tell he is not trying to actually fight me. I get irritated. Main stone says, "This is for the safety of many so you can punish him. Do so."

Needing no other encouragement, I thrash him until he just collapses. He is taken to the infirmary. I say, "Anyone else want to treat me as if I am fragile?"

Strong fights

The rest of the day is spent on intense lessons. However, as I am learning, I only get through three people. I am too tired to do more. I am glad when grandpa calls dinnertime. Again, the main stone waits until I am lying on my bed to heal me. I again dream of the matches until I can do them with ease, being healed in between each dream set of the three matches. The next day, I do more training, as I am doing so, I see my sisters huddle together. I wonder what they are up to, but the main stone has again shut my magic off. When I finish the training set against the one individual, I go over to them asking, "What are you up to?"

Mertha says, "If grandpa lets us, we think it is time you have a match against us."

Grandpa says, "Alright. All of you go all out, just do not kill each other."

Orvalina says, "Not a chance of us going that far grandpa. Fighting Sam will increase all of our skill levels. She heals faster than we do."

I say, "Well then, what are the match terms?"

They tell me it will be me against the three of them at once. If any knock me down, they win. However, to win, I have to knock them all down. We set boundaries and leaving the area is a forfeit. I lose if they have not been knocked down by dinner the next day and we start just after breakfast and none of us have lunch. Since it is dinner time now, we go eat. The main stone again heals me as I lay down for the night and repeats today's training until I have mastered it while I sleep.

After breakfast, my mortal family goes to the training fields. All guards are again there. This time the wateries are protecting the capital. The guards form a circle around the area my sisters and I chose as an arena. One says, "No offense Princess, I hope they knock some since in you."

I say, "You are next."

My sisters and I fight all day. I manage to avoid about half of their attacks. They avoid all of mine. Just before dinner, I land on my back. They instantly stop. I sigh as I get to my feet then before anyone leaves, I ask, "Rematch tomorrow?"

They nod. We eat and rest. Again, the main stone heals me as I lay on my bed and repeats the match all night. I am exhausted when I wake up. Main stone says, "About time I got you to this point. Now I can teach you how to use an energy spear without others knowing."

I say, "Teach me."

Main stone chimes, "Energy is mine from all times and places in my authority."

I repeat that to find myself ready for today. I join my family for breakfast. Seeing me healed my sisters flinch. I grin asking, "Ready to fight yet?"

They say, "Let us eat first. We did agree to no lunch in the match."

I say, "As you wish."

After breakfast, we go to the training fields. The crystal warriors are protecting the nation today. It takes me ten minutes to knock all three of them down and I was not hit once. Once they concede, I attack the one who said he wished they taught me a lesson. However, I only knock him off his feet as well. Then I stand down. Diana says, "Sire Sam, I must get home. My people are going to stress if I stay away much longer."

Mertha says, "Yes, I am on limited time to assure my people they are safe as well."

Orvalina says, "That makes three of us. See you all next year."

They salute me and leave. Grandpa says, "Take the rest of the day off Sam. You have done very well these past few days."

I say, "Thank you. Una, Pegasus, lets go for a ride."

My unicorns come over to me. Mom asks, "Where are you going Sam?"

I reply, "I told you that when I showed you my colors."

Mom says, "Stay safe."

I say, "Of course. Be back at dinner."

Then I command my unicorns into a gallop before the guards can react. I ride out into the clearing then slow them and go into the forest at their walking pace. Once I cannot see the city walls as if I were a human, I use crystal magic to travel to that world. Orvalina instantly salutes me. I visit with the people for an hour letting them all know I care. After that, I go to the dragon nation. Diana submits to me. I spend an hour with them to let them know I care about them as well. From there I ride Una while Pegasus is beside her. Main stone says, "Ask your unicorns how old they are."

I do that. Pegasus replies, "Mistress, I am seven. Una will be seven tomorrow."

Main stone says, "Adults. Ask why they both chose you."

I obey. Pegasus replies, "I chose you as you are strong as my mate is said to be."

Una says, "I chose you as you are kind as my mate is said to be."

I say, "You are both strong and kind. Thank you for thinking so highly of me to choose me."

They look at each other. Una's horn glows. Pegasus nods. His horn glows and Una nods. I wonder what is going on. Main stone says, "They are communicating with each other in private. Do not ask about their conversation. I doubt you want to hear personal conversations of those close to your parents age in unicorn equivalent. If you ask, they would have to tell you, even if you gave them the option not to."

I say, "Drop me off above the mer nation, but make sure no humans see it. Then you both land on the shore of the nation that is home. I will meet you there and we will go home where I will treat you both for the fun ride."

They nod. Moments later, we are above the mer nation, in the sky past human sight. Pegasus says, "Wait mistress. Humans below us."

I listen but prepare myself for a fast drop when they let me know it is safe to. Five minutes pass before Una says, "Alright mistress, be safe. See you on shore."

Conversation with a sea dragon

Dropping, I force myself not to change into dragon as I do not want to scare the wateries or the mers. My body objects to this. The force of hitting the water is painful. The pain triggers my mer form and I am instantly fine. Knowing better then staying near the surface as a mer, I swim down fast. Two minutes later, I am outside of the cave Meme uses to hide her water force dragon from many. Wondering why it allows me near it, I go into the cave. It does not even toss a water ball at me. I ask about that.

It says, "Peacemaker, none in the protection or healing forces harm or even attempt to harm those who chose his last names. It is against our laws. Those such as me are in the protection forces. Phoenixes are also in the protection forces. You chose sire's last name. We cannot even attack you. Meme does not know we cannot even attack you. The only reason I would toss a water ball at you is to protect you."

I ask, "What about when mom was carrying my siblings and I?"

It replies, "Pure dragon. I was not sure of."

I say, "Diana is my sister. So is Orvalina and Mertha. I do not want any of them harmed."

It says, "As Peacemaker asks. Meme is coming, so I think we should change subject."

We do that. Moments later, Meme joins us. She says, "Sam, why did my pet not threaten you? I wonder as you have never been here before and I do not detect its water ball remnants."

I ask, "How would I know?"

Meme asks, "Tark, why did you not test Sam?"

Tark says, "I know she is safe. Her sister and mother are. There is no reason to doubt her strength as little Mertha submits to her."

Meme accepts it. I wonder if that was why it did not attack me. Then I know that somehow the last name the main stone gave me is the reason many are submitting to me even just meeting me. Tark said I had chose his last name with respect. Was he talking about Kar? Why am I not afraid to say the name in any other way besides addressing him as king? Why do the Ancients- at least Poem call me king? Who was Tark referencing?

I wonder all of that while I swim closer to the mer nation. Main stone chimes, "Was not Kar that Tark referenced. It is the Emperor he respects. I gave you one of the Emperor's seven last names besides all of the magic last names. You just have to prove you can handle the responsibilities that come with it to keep that last name and you will prove it as long as you obey my commands. Only us immortality shards have that last name until almost all of the shards are gathered. There are not many more, but I get into the kings' rank before those without the shard get the name. The only thing is are you the one who carries me back to the empire's center or is it someone else. Are you willing to let me lead you to greatness?"

Willing? I picked up an elfin stone with a strange voice and somehow trust it. I am scared of the things it says and people's responses, yet I would not willingly give up my elfin stone. It is my second one, yet I cannot replicate it as I can my first one. Nothing seems to look or feel right. It just does not turn out. Maybe that is because I had to lock most of my magic to stay hidden here among the mortals. I do not know. I decide to try later, after I can use the elf magic again. At that moment, I reach the mer nation. It took me four minutes from the surface. Ann needs twenty. I know I will make her proud.

I visit with the mers for an hour then go to the surface. There I ride Una back home with Pegasus beside me. I hear people questioning why my parents and grandparents let a five-year-old leave on her own so I change everyone's memories to not know I left. The castle staff think I went to my room for a couple hours and the town does not remember seeing me at all today. I put my unicorns in the stables and groom them good. Then I give them both apples, oats and water. From there, as the memory mix took effect just a bit sooner then I thought it would, I crystal travel into my new bedroom. I did to much today. I drop on my bed asleep.

Main stone chimes, "Energy spears and time spaces. Energy from all times and places under my command to me now."

I wake up fully alert. It shocks me to see only a minute has passed. Or was it a day? Main stone says, "One minute to gain energy anytime you need it. Because you picked me up, you can go seven years on very little sleep."

Many fights

Wow. I go to the training fields and practice what I have been taught. A warrior comes by. I challenge him. We fight all out and I win. I stop when he is panting and thank him for the match. Days pass by as I defeat one person after another in an all-out match without grandpa near. The guards then go against me two at a time. A week later, I am able to handle that. They do three on one. I take a week to be able to win that way. Four on one. Then five against me. It keeps building until I can match them all at once. It takes them a month to challenge me again. This time the one I punished for taking it easy on me is recovered enough and got his courage back to join them. I still win. Every time we match, I thank whoever is against me as they are going all out. I know such will help me stay safe and keep my people safe without the use of magic.

The only problem I have is that my eyes were bright blue before mom forced me to join the mortals and they are red now. I want them back at my birth color. Main stone says, "They will get there before you rejoin the immortals because you want them so. Once you get back to the immortals, your eye color does not change as easily as it does here."

I wonder how long that will be. It is one of the days I have taken completely off for months. I am sitting alone in the high tower, just under the bell. I know my descendants might have use for magic weapons, so I make some. I also make a shield and a ring. On all I place the empire's symbol. Most of the nations' symbols to be hidden until they are unlocked. In the ring I place a beacon to bring the holder to this nation. Then I lock them in a box at the side of the tower. Main stone chimes, "Items made by a Peacemaker are only safe for the Peacemakers to touch without permission. With permission the holder will have nightmares until the item is returned to a Peacemaker!"

Questions

The empire's symbol, including the star form I do not have lights up around me and the items I made then vanish. Instantly I am drained. I wake up days later. My immortal mom asks, "How are you Sam?"

I ask, "What happened?"

Mom says, "You passed out a few days ago. Why?"

I say, "I must have over did myself. What do the mortals know of it?"

Mom replies at the same time as the main stone chimes, "Nothing."

Main stone says, "I kept them from knowing it."

Mom says, "I do not know how, but no one here seemed to notice your absence. I kept hidden from them and they seem to think you were there all along. I do not get how that is possible."

I say, "It is me mom. I image project in extreme need. Mortals would never know the difference."

Mom says, "Only I seemed to notice. At the time I felt your energy drop, the Ancients were walking by. They all smiled. Stars said, 'I wondered how long it would take her to use enough energy to need sleep.' Poem said, 'Stronger than Kar's energy draw.' Mer asked, 'Do you think---' At that I heard no more as they were gone."

I sigh, "They were talking of someone very important to them, yet they let you overhear it…. why would they consider me important?"

Mom asks, "You think they were talking about you?"

I sigh, "They smiled at the precise moment you felt my energy drop. They were talking of me. To perfect on timing to be anyone else."

Poem shows up asking, "You try to stress us child?"

I ask, "Why would I try? Why are you here?"

Mom gasps, "Sam! Be respectful to Ancient Poem."

Poem says, "Madam relax. I took no offense to her questions. As to why you would try…all have. I am here as you were talking about my group of friends."

I ask, "Why do you think I am special?"

Poem replies, "You know that."

I ask, "Why would I be?"

Poem says, "You know that as well."

I ask, "Why would it matter?"

Poem says, "You also know that."

I ask, "Why do you respect me?"

Poem says, "You know that too."

I say, "I hear it, yet I do not understand it. What makes that so different?"

Poem says, "I believe you have seen or heard the answer to that also."

Mom asks, "Miss Ancient, why do you respect my daughter?"

Poem asks, "Does the young one know?"

Main stone chimes, "Of course we do, Cella. We cannot tell her though. The knowledge would hurt Zeyla. Sam, just shrug."

I do that. Poem says, "If you do not know, you will one day. Zeyla leave."

Mom obeys. Poem says, "See you sometime."

She is gone as well. Main stone says, "I am the reason people respect you even just meeting you. I will lead you into the kings' ranks. If you do really well, you will not only meet the Emperor, but serve him as well."

Instantly I want to serve such a person that the main stone respects when it draws respect from so many. Having slept for a few days, I go train. My mortal parents and grandparents join me there. Mom asks, "How well do you do in the training Sam?"

Main stone says, "Do not brag."

Punishment

I say, "I do fair. I want to increase the difficulty for me but doubt the guards will do so without grandpa encouraging them."

Grandpa asks, "What do you have in mind?"

I say, "My fighting against them while blindfolded."

Grandpa says, "Let us see your skills then."

All the guards are called together. I fight them and win. At that, grandpa says, "Very well Sam, you can blindfold yourself in fights. I expect the guards not to kill you and to stop if you fall until you get back on your feet fully. If you end up in the infirmary, it is your own fault."

I say, "Yes grandpa. May I go for a ride in town without guards?"

Grandpa sighs, "At least we know you can defend yourself. Go ahead."

I get my unicorns and go for a ride through town. As usual, I am riding Una and Pegasus is walking beside me. The town people all salute me. I smile at them. Halfway through town, a little girl of four, steps out of the crowd. She asks, "Why two horses Princess?"

Pegasus says, "Young miss is too close to me."

I say, "I give them exercise. Why do you ask?"

She asks, "Can I ride one?"

I ask, "Do you know how to ride?"

Shaking her head, she asks, "Would I be allowed to learn?"

I ask, "What is your name?"

She replies, "Patricia."

I say, "Nice to meet you Patricia. Let me check with grandpa before answering your question. Right now, though, Pegasus has taken offence to how close you are to him without my permission first."

Patricia asks, "Can I touch him? I love horses. They are so beautiful and strong."

I say, "That I will allow. Behave Pegasus."

Pegasus nods. Patricia rubs Pegasus' nose. My unicorn is calm until she gets to close to his horn. At that he snorts and backs away from her. I say, "Pegasus has a sensitive space and you got to close to it. Calm down Pegasus."

Coming close to me, Pegasus replies, "I am calm mistress. Child would ask about my horn if she feels it. I cannot let her touch it."

Una's muscles get tense. I ask, "What is wrong Una?"

My unicorn replies, "Danger. Not for us. Somewhere close. Someone is in danger."

Una moves in small circles. I let her lead. A moment later, Una runs back the direction we came. Two minutes later, she says, "The child! Grab her."

I ask, "What child?"

Seconds later, we round a corner. In that instant, I see a child in front of me falling as a tree branch snaps. I react and grab the girl as we dart pass. I hold her as Una slows. We loop back to see a massive branch in the road. It would have landed on the girl I hold had we not gotten to her in time. The branch is heavy even though it is diseased enough to break under her pressure as I am sure she was climbing on it.

Seeing the branch, the girl says, "Thank you miss!"

I have Una lower as we are to high to safely set the girl down. Once Una obeys, I set the girl on her feet saying, "I am glad I was near enough to help."

She hugs me hard. Her parents come over expressing their gratitude that I saved their daughter. I reply, "Glad I was near enough to do so. You are safe, there is no reason to hug me so hard."

Easing up on her hug she asks, "Can I learn fighting? I know you could teach me as no guards are with you today."

I reply, "Once you are five, you could start learning. Grandpa has that age restriction on there as most do not know how to follow directions before that. You learn against the lowest warrior first as would any working your way up to the top fighter."

She asks, "Who is the top fighter? How skilled are you?"

I say, "I am fair. Decent enough grandpa let me come into town without guards. Ask grandpa who is the best fighter he has."

She says, "Thank you again for saving me."

I say, "Do not worry about it."

Main stone says, "James tried to locate energy transfer Una did pulling from you to keep the child safe. When your energy was drawn from, you automatically draw from the closest energy spear."

I silently wonder, "What do we do about that?"

Main stone asks, "Is the child willing to repay you?"

I say, "There is actually something you can do for me."

She asks, "What is that?"

I say, "Someone might ask how you avoided the branch. Just claim that it happened so fast you are not sure. After all are you sure how I reacted so fast? It is important that one has no idea I am a part of it. Do you think you can convince that one it was just you without lying?"

She says, "I will give it a try."

I nod saying, "Una, Pegasus, let us continue our walk."

We move off. Main stone says, "By the way, you disobeyed me by bragging."

I wonder, "How so?"

Main stone says, "By asking to be blindfolded after saying you were fair you said you were stronger than the rest. You then proved that. Child you move so fast because of me. Now you will hurt because I will not help you again."

I think, "Please do not leave me."

Main stone says, "No, your minor disobedience is not enough to get me to leave you. It is however enough for me not to help you in the matches again. You learn them as you did before."

I finish my ride, take care of my unicorns and go find grandpa. I say, "Grandpa, we need to have the trees in town tested for diseases. A branch broke with a girl my size on it. The branch was big enough to hold an adult but diseased. I was near enough to save her life without dragon help, but I do not know how many trees need treated or removed."

Dad is nearby so asks, "Did you ask for help from any called flower?"

I question, "What right would I have?"

Dad says, "Rose Flower once scared Ann. What did she say that scared you so much Ann?"

Mom replies, "Asked if I was from my nation. With your having shown me the museum two days before that I panicked. Only that nation and my home nation are animal talkers. It is rare. At least she made sure only I heard her."

Dad says, "Anyways, go ask her if Hesta Honeyeater and its family are well then mention the tree issue. Those called Flower are best to take care of issues with plants."

I ask, "What right do I have?"

Ann says, "Probably none. However, they need to know of issues you discovered on plants they might be taking care of."

I reply, "Alright. Where does Rose Flower live?"

Fairy help

Dad tells me the area she usually stands in. I walk out. When I get to the area in town that Rose lives in, main stone chimes, "We could do so ourselves except that would alert the ones who are testing you of your whereabouts and force a failure. I leave you if you fail. I will not force you to separate from me without a serious offence. Remember, if you disobey my commands, you suffer more than I can help you with. Third house on the right. Flowers in the windows is fairy home. I know as no other flowers are growing as big. That is daily fairy care."

I go knock on that door. A girl of I guess eleven answers. She asks, "What do you want Diadon?"

Making sure she is Rose, I say, "Rose, I am an animal talker. I know you care for plants. I was riding in town a bit a go and rescued a girl about my age from being crushed by a thick tree branch that broke under her. It was diseased. I do not know how many trees are infected, but it is unsafe to have them infected and not cured. If they cannot be treated, we need to remove them for everyone's safety. Mom told me you are good with plants and would be able to let us know which ones to remove."

Rose questions, "What are you not saying?"

I ask, "Can you help Rose?"

Rose says, "Of course I can. Why are you asking? You identified yourself as one of two groups, yet I know your father and grandmother are Donics."

I say, "That is true. Remember though, mom is an animal talker. I inherited both."

Rose asks, "What else?"

I say, "Well, opposites did not handle tight spaces, so a crystal magic helped mom out and named her heir. I have that also."

Rose asks, "What else?"

Main stone says, "Command her using your last name."

I quietly wonder, "How?"

Main stone replies, "In a commanding tone tell her your last name then order her to obey you. No magic disobeys it when you are in the right. Saving lives is right. After she submits to you, have her talk to you alone."

I command, "My name is Peacemaker! You will obey me."

It takes three minutes for Rose to drop into a position of respect then she sighs, "What is it you ask of me?"

I say, "Let us talk alone."

We go into her home. She asks, "Miss, why did I respond to your last name? I did not want to."

Main stone says, "Tell her then make her promise never to share it with anyone even guardians."

I say, "Rose, my last name has been recognized by the Ancients as a king over them. It is then right that I can command anyone in the empire under them if it is to help others and save lives. I asked you to check the trees because if I do, I fail the test I am being put through to gain the right to lead so many. I then would not get to be a king and lose any chance at the king's rank. My parents are immortals and made me join Matt and Ann as their child asking that I treat the royals here as my family. That is why I do. You are forbidden to share our conversation with anyone even guardians."

Rose asks, "Do you consider me wise?"

I say, "I cannot give you the title of any magic that everyone does not realize I have; mer, dragon, and crystal. That is why I ask for your help with the trees. If you help, I can pass my test and eventually become a king of the empire. I promise that one of your family will join the immortals Princess Rose Flower."

Rose says, "That will do, my king."

I say, "I am changing everyone's memories to where I had asked you to check the health of the trees and you agreed for everyone's safety. That is all they know. Treat me the way you did before we talked as only my parents, the empire and the Ancients know where I am. Only two other guardians know of my existence and one of those is who is testing me. The other one is there to teach me when I get past the one who is testing me."

Rose says, "Alright sire. Take care of yourself. One more question. Are you an immortal?"

I say, "Yes. I am trapped with mortals until I pass my test. If it only takes me one round, I can make it to becoming a king of the empire. I do not know past that."

We walk outside together. I see the memory mix happen for everyone near us. Rose says, "You asked me to tell you what trees are beyond help. Let us walk together. I will test them, and you get a correct list."

I nod. We walk together. The first tree we come to Rose leans close to it. I think she is smelling it. I know she is just fooling humans on how she knows which ones are good. She can feel it as I can. Hers might be weaker than mine, but all fairies know by feel how the plants are doing. She says, "Healthy."

We move on. Tree after tree we go to. Down one street and up another. The only tree in the capital that needs to be removed is the one that broke. As we get near it, Rose stops twenty feet back and shakes her head saying, "Poisoned. Not useful for anything anymore. Must be burned at high flame intensity. I smell it even here. Excuse me, I do not feel well."

She walks off. I silently ask, "Main stone, would you move me into complete fairy?"

Main stone replies, "Others would learn you have fairy magic."

I say, "Not. You can hide me from everyone even others with the invisible stones then you can hide me for a few minutes in total fairy."

Main stone says, "You will get sick."

I silently say, "I need to know how strong the fire needs to be. Being a full fairy will let me know that."

Main stone says, "Very well. Bev, a king over you will need your help soon. We are hidden from everyone but the Ancients of the empire and its kings."

Then I am fully a fairy. I feel sick in seconds. The only fire that will take care of it is mine. However, I need to be healed first and Bev would hurt coming here. I move away from the tree as fast as I can until I do not feel the radiating poison coming from it. I say, "Bev please help me."

Rose was close enough to hear me. She whispers, "Me too please Ancient Flower."

I see Rose pass out. Bev joins us. I say, "Heal her first!"

Bev nods and heals Rose. Then Bev heals me. As soon as I am healed, main stone chimes, "Leave Bev. We need to go back to how everyone thinks we are so we can lower the hidden field."

So, Bev leaves. Rose asks, "Are you alright?"

I reply, "Fine. I am just resting. That tree is the only one needing to be removed?"

Rose says, "The only one in the capital. I asked the other flower folk to check out the plants near them. They will finish as soon as they can and let me know the results. I will let you know."

I say, "Alright. I will let grandpa know about the trees we checked."

After I let grandpa know the report, I whisper, "The rainbow dragon will burn the tree tonight. The rainbow mermaid will make sure nothing else gets burned. Tomorrow, I will be staying in my room longer than normal."

Grandpa says, "Keep safe."

I nod. After everyone has gone to bed, I change into my dragon appearance, turn invisible and fly out of my bedroom window. I go burn the tree while making sure the fire is contained. I wait until the fire is dying down before going back to my room and taking human looks. The next morning, I wake up to the town talking of the tree being burned mysteriously. I flip over and get some more rest. At lunch I join my mortal family. Grandpa asks, "Feeling well Sam?"

Nodding, I reply, "I just stayed up a bit later than I should have. I am fine."

⸺ ⟋⟍⟋∘⟍∘⟋∘⟋∘⟋⟍ ⸺

Blindfolded fights

The next day is my birthday. The following day is my first blindfolded fight. The main stone does as it had at first and lets me get beat. A one on one battle. The warrior stops whenever I fall until I am back on my feet. I pass out before dinner. Main stone then says, "Now I heal you and you learn the moves he does."

By morning I am completely healed. Healer Janice Donic is surprised I healed so fast. I say, "Do not barter unless I am still hurt the next morning. I am joining my family for breakfast and then I am training. I need to be able to fight."

She says, "Be careful sire."

I say, "Careful is for the weak. You know I am not weak."

She sighs. I join my family for breakfast. They are stunned as well. Then I go to the training fields and win against the one I battled yesterday. However, I lose against the next rank. Main stone again heals me at night and teaches me the battle. Months pass by in this manner. Then I do two on one battles. Another couple of months then I am against three. It builds until I am doing all warriors against me again. After a month of them losing every day they refuse to fight me.

I will be seven soon. As they did last year my sisters join our family for my birthday and stay a couple days to fight. This year the warriors ask them to join the fight against me. My sisters agree. It is the best fight I have had. My sisters make it intense. They are the last ones standing though I tried to knock them out first. They are good warriors themselves being far stronger than grandpa's warriors. I know they realize that I am better able to protect them and their people if I can fight strong without magic, so they do their best to help me learn it.

The next day, I go into the forest alone. I ask the tiger pack leader if it will race me. We race many times that day. After our races, I bring its pack a lot of meat. They agree to continue the agreement they made with my father through my lifetime and tell me that if I ever want to race them again to let them know. Pack leader nudges me. I decide it would be easier if the pack leader could communicate with anyone it wanted to, so I give it some fairy magic to be passed on the leader rights. Tiger leader thanks me for it with the promise not to harm me or any offspring I have. Not able to tell the pack leader completely apart from the rest, I change its fur coloring from orange as the pack is to white. That somehow changed the eye color it has from brown to one orange and one blue. I know it is also something the pack leader will have for many years.

A few days later, grandpa asks to see how well I am doing on my training. I reply, "Fighting against many while blindfolded."

Grandpa says, "Let us see then."

I say, "If you want to see that you will have to find some willing to fight me. These cowards will not."

Captain says, "We have more common since than to get into a guaranteed losing battle young sire. We all went against you and even with your sisters here joining us, we could not win, and you were blindfolded! Only a fool takes up that challenge knowing your strength."

I say, "I try."

Grandpa says, "Good. I will never have to worry about your safety after I die. You will make a good ruler one day Sam."

I say, "I will do my best to be good for those under my command."

The next day I am alone in the throne room sitting upside down as my normal when Zeffron in the female looks joins me. Zeffron asks, "Why do you sit that way Sam?"

I reply, "It helps me think."

Zeffron says, "Weird. See you later weird one."

Then I am alone again. I do not care if Zeffron thinks I am weird. Sitting this way does help me think. That is think of my birth parents. I wonder how they are, but I cannot ask and cannot even have mom come visit me here. My eighth birthday is usual. One warrior asks, "How did you get so good at fighting young sire?"

I reply, "I train a lot. I listen to the breathing patterns around me. I love to be challenged."

The warriors try refusing to fight, when my sisters come, but my sisters command them to join the fight against me. The guards complain when they lose. I say, "Thank you for obeying my sisters and fighting me today. Next year, sisters, you are on your own. I will not continue to force them to join us when they cannot even help the three of you to have a better chance."

Losing grandpa

They nod and leave. A few months later, grandpa takes ill. I instantly step up and become acting head of state. Months pass by but grandpa does not recover. He dies days before I turn ten. Without any complaints or arguments, I am crowned king the next day. The announcer called it out that it was my grandfather's last wish that I be crowned king and not queen to keep me and the nation safer. As soon as I am crowned king, I tell my people I do not approve of slavery and therefore I was decreeing all slaves are to be freed immediately.

That is obeyed. I know some might do so just of fear of what I might do if they disobeyed as I fight so well, but that does not matter. Having no slaves in any place I have authority over is what matters to me. I hear Zeffron call out, "There will be an explosion in the wealth of the land, so none regret setting the slaves free. As long as Sam's family rules there it will prosper. The opposite will happen if someone tries to take that land from the Peacemakers."

I call out, "I wish everyone long lives, peace and happiness. Thank you for accepting me as your king."

Not sure who starts it, but I soon hear a chant of 'Long live King Peacemaker' ring out. I let it continue for a couple of minutes thinking of the one that the main stone gave me the last name of and wishing him a long life as well. Then I thank my people for their well wishes and go into my castle. I sit on the throne upright with my arms wrapped around my knees unable to cry for the lost life because it would hurt many.

Hours pass by as I sit there processing the pain of losing grandpa. After a bit, Ann, Matt and Grandma join me and comfort me. After an hour of their company, I tell them I am going for a ride. Then I get my unicorns and do so. Knowing I will exhaust myself without help, I set out to find the three honest people I chose years ago as my informants. I will now ask them what I am sure they will accept. They know me though they might think it was a dream. I start in the northern most town. I land an hour from it, get off Una and give my unicorns their treats. After I make sure my unicorns are taken care of, I change my looks to someone who would not be questioned by anyone that is old enough to be traveling alone. Then I walk into the town.

Going to the town square, I sit on a park bench and wait. Minutes later, my informant comes by. I fall into step beside her. I say, "Morning miss, remember me?"

She replies, "Yes miss, come to my home."

I follow her there and then ask her to inform me of any events, concerns or rumors she hears of. After she agrees, I go to the eastern most town and repeat the process. I follow that by the southern most town. My three helpers all agreed to serve me as informants. Done with that, I go home. After taking care of Una and Pegasus once more, I go train again.

A few years go by and only my sisters will battle me. I only see them a few days a year around my birthday. I am board. Another year and I cannot stand being so board anymore. Main stone says, "Issue a challenge then."

Challenge

I go to the library. Alone here, I say, "Guardian Zeffron, I want to know how to get others to fight me."

Zeffron in female appearance as always is around females comes. Zeffron says, "Hold a competition for skilled warriors. Do not have them know that you are the strongest fighter in the land. Disguise yourself. Also promise a reward for anyone that could defeat the strongest in your land."

I thank Zeffron for the input, then call a meeting with my advisors and guards. Once everyone is gathered, I say, "I want a competition. Please find skilled fighters. Willing to take on a strong fighter, the best in the land. If they managed to defeat the fighter Sam, the unmarried queen of the land would reward them for it. Under no circumstances is it to be mentioned that the fighter Sam is a female, let alone the queen. Those that want to see if they could defeat this warrior are to be brought here for a good competition. No one is to know that my name is Sam or that I am the only one in the entire nation with that name. You are to simply say the Queen Peacemaker wants to see if there is anyone stronger then the fighter Sam. When you all return with the fighters in a year's time you should only address me as Queen, Queen Peacemaker, or Peacemaker until after the competition is over and the fighters leave. Bring as many as you can by the time that I am sixteen. Spread the news of the competition as far as you can. Maybe someone in another nation can give me a good match."

Captain of the guard says, "More as a lot of fools."

Everyone laughs. I smile saying, "At least they will be willing to fight me."

The guards laugh, "They will learn better."

I say, "Perhaps. Here are official letters. Please go."

The guards all salute me and leave. My sisters show up. Tomorrow is my fifteenth birthday. Diana says, "We heard that. Any who accept are fools."

I question, "Are you three up to challenging?"

They fight me. I win again. I sigh. My sisters apologize for not being able to help me get stronger. I tell them to not worry about it. Orvalina asks, "Why send out all the guards?"

I say, "Spread the word the most."

Days later, they leave. I make the announcement of the competition to my nation. The result is that a few days before I turn sixteen, the capital becomes crowded. It gets much more crowded as the warriors return with foreign competitors the day after I turn sixteen. All of the foreigners are male. I have them all gather on the castle grounds to eat. The feast they all enjoy. After everyone has ate, I stand saying, "Thank you all for coming. As I had my messengers say, I invited everyone here for a competition. There is a prize for any who win against my strongest fighter, Sam. All interested in competing should line up. I need names and want a bit of information about you and why you think you could defeat Sam. The order the fights will be in will be determined randomly. The competition starts tomorrow, and you will not see me again until the competition is over."

All the foreigners line up. I get their information then leave them to interact having my guards show my guests to rooms when they wanted rest. Then I go to the library. There Zeffron joins me asking, "What do you plan on giving as the prize?"

Pleased about the number of fights I will have I reply, "If more than one, money. If only one it depends on the person. If that one asks about the fighter, I would double the amount of money if he does want the reward or if he tells me to keep the reward, I will give him my life and respect."

Zeffron says, "You will lose your freedom if you bow to anyone. Are you sure about this?"

I reply, "I am sure. I do not take this decision lightly. All married males will go first in the competition. They will be concerned about their families so easier to defeat. They should get back to their families anyways. I need to go over the list now and assign the order to fight in."

Zeffron leaves. I freeze time so everyone can get enough rest and I can get the order figured out. As my sisters are here, I have them entertain my guests for breakfast along with our parents. I also ask them to have the announcer meet me in the library. There I give him the list and tell him the instructions letting him know to call me fighter Sam, that I would not talk and would not eat lunch. He nods and asks, "What disguise will you use?"

Loss of freedom

I say, "I will have a disguise that will make me appear as a male with thin armor on. Allow the fighters to use any weapon, armor and anything else they want. Feed everyone well. Whatever they want to eat, or drink is fine."

He says, "That might burden the people."

I say, "No. I have been preparing for this for enough time to not burden the people yet allow everyone to eat good now."

He accepts it. I look out the window waiting until everyone is on the field and has their order numbers. Even the princes and kings that have come are there. Then I take my disguise and walk out joining them. Reaching the arena, I wonder if any are skilled enough to defeat me. I stop at the announcer whispering, "Let us start."

Someone asks, "Where is the queen of the nation?"

Captain of my guard replies, "I assume she just finished talking with fighter Sam."

Announcer calls out, "These matches are to be untimed. The first one to knock the opponent down three times will be the winner. Sam is to only use a wooden rod and the armor that is currently on our strong fighter. The challengers can use any armor and weapon they want. One on one battles. Low number first."

The fight starts. Many of my people are watching along with all the competitors that I am not currently against. I fight one after another all morning. When I hear people whispering about being hungry, I raise my hand signaling for a break. Grandma says, "Warrior Sam has declared a break time so everyone can have lunch. Please enjoy the feast our staff made for everyone."

Minutes later, everyone is seated, and lunch is served. I do not eat while using magic, so I reject food as I must keep my disguise. Most places do not allow females to fight. I know people notice and question my action as they whisper about it. They think I will be weaker in the afternoon. I defeat them all as well. Then dinner is served, and I leave them going to my rooms to have the special dinner my family prepared for me. The meal will bring my magic energy levels back up to normal. Being alone keeps the competitors from learning my gender and then refusing to fight because of it.

Day after day, week after week, and month after month, it is much the same. I have defeated three-fourths without even being knocked off my feet once. Then the fighters start being more careful, and I do not go through as many, but I have still not been knocked down even once.

Many months have gone by. I defeated all I fought against. This is so boring. Is there no one that can give me a challenge? Main stone chimes, "There are some. My equals, their spouses, Sire and his family, all of their spouses, and the one you choose as your forever love."

I am glad to know at least some can put up a good match without getting hurt. There are five fighters left. My seventeenth birthday is fast approaching. These fighters are a prince, a baker, a shoemaker, a potter, and a glass maker. I decide to give them time to decide if they still wanted to fight. I walk over to the announcer and whisper, "Give them a chance to back out of the competition."

Announcer calls out, "Fighter Sam wants to know if anyone wishes to drop out of the competition."

The baker and shoemaker drop out. It is dinner time, so everyone has a good meal. I go to my room. There my sisters join me and whisper that their people are feeling drained. I cannot continue using so much energy. I have already decided that I want three all day events, so I finish the day before my birthday. I ask, "Sisters, please make me armor that would appear the same as the disguise I have used when I wear it then."

They do. The next morning, I have the announcer call out the change that these matches would-be all-day events. The challenger only had to knock fighter Sam down three times the whole day, to win, only loosing if they failed to do so.

First up is the potter. I knock him down so many times that by the end of the day he is limping. I have not even been hit off my feet once. The next day is the glass maker. He is knocked down ten times by days end. I have not been knocked down at all. This is very boring. At least it will be over after tomorrow. With the following day being my seventeenth birthday.

The prince that is left has spent every day watching me. He told me he is single and nineteen. I think he has some physical appeal to some, but I have no interest in him. I do not know him enough to even consider anything other than friendship. The last day of the competition is finally here. We are tied at lunch. He also refuses to eat. Why? He has ate for lunch all year, yet now he refuses. What is going on?"

I am distracted wondering about his skipping the meal. As the day goes on, I wonder if he is stronger than he lets on. Main stone tells me I should focus, but I do not. Just before dinnertime, I land on my back hard. He had managed to knock me down. I quickly flip over so no one sees me in pain. I know my magic is disrupted and it is dangerous for me to continue fighting, but I refuse to give up. I stand and swing my rod at him. I land on my back again. I try to knock him down only to fail the challenge as he succeeds in knocking me off my feet for the third time. I get up and hurry off so I can heal before my family joins me in my quarters.

As I walk away, I hear my guards say, "The reward will be given out tomorrow."

The prince says, "I do not care about the reward, is your fighter-Sam fine?"

My guards reply, "We are sure that Sam is fine, just hating losing. Sam has never lost before. Not since Sam was trained anyways."

I meet Zeffron just outside of the library on my way in there as I will not stay alert if I go to my quarters. Zeffron says a healing spell. Main stone says, "Weak spell as Zeffron assumes you are not as strong as even Meme. I will heal you as I did years ago. Zeffron will assume it is the spell. Rainbow healing."

As Zeffron leaves, I feel fine. I know that was the main stone far more then Zeffron's little spell. I finish up my daily tasks, tell my family that the competition is over and get some rest. The next day I am seventeen. I dress in my queenly best because of it and go to the fields where everyone is having breakfast. All, even the visitors stand and salute me. I know the visitors are just following the customs my people have adopted since I gained the throne. They all sit after I sit in the place prepared for me. The prince that had defeated me asks, "Is your fighter Sam ok?"

I respond, "Sam is fine."

He asks, "Can I meet this Sam without the armor?"

I reply, "After breakfast when the ones that lost leave."

Breakfast is quiet after that. I realize they all hoped to meet the one they were against, but I have zero desire to tell them. I would not tell him if he had not defeated me and asked. Someone else asks, "When does he get his reward?"

Another asks, "What is the reward?"

I answer, "The reward is between me and the winner. It will be given out when everyone of them that lost have left."

It is not hard to notice that many of them do not believe there is a reward for the winner now, but they go with acting as if they accept my words. After the meal, the losers thank me for my generous hospitality and leave. It is just my people (mostly my staff), me and the prince that had defeated me here. I wonder which prize I will give him. I know I could end up being a slave for years and single as there is zero chance that I would ask for permission to date. This decision could affect me for years. It would last the rest of his life.

He asks again, "Might I meet the fighter Sam without the armor?"

I ask, "Sir, do you even think about the reward?"

He answers, "You can keep the reward, I just want to make sure, for myself, that the fighter Sam is fine."

I see him looking around trying to figure out who he went against, but he never would. My decision on how to treat the winner was firm, and though I am not happy now, I kneel before him saying in magic common, "Then my king has my respect."

His wondering what I said is clear as he faces me. I hear my people gasp and see them sit in moments. I hurt for them as they trust me so much, they would follow me anywhere and not disrespect me even in my statement that a near stranger would rule over us. He says, "Why would a queen bow to a prince? I do not understand."

My parents and grandma join us just before he asked. Mom says, "You must have earned her respect. I have never known her to submit as such to anyone. Not even her grandfather, the king that ruled this land before her. How did you manage it?"

He responds, "I am not sure. I asked to meet the fighter-Sam to make sure that he was fine. She said something, and when I turned to ask what was said she was bowing to me."

Mom asks, "You asked to meet the one you fought against?"

I see that she thinks I might have told everyone that I was the fighter, but I had no intention of doing so. He says, "Yes. Why does my asking cause such a strange reaction?"

Mom says, "Because the only one that is called Sam in this entire nation is the queen. She is the one you fought."

Facing me, he asks, "Is that true?"

Nodding, I reply, "Yes, I am the strongest fighter in my land. Please do not hold it against me that I hid my identity from everyone. I know most would have refused to fight if they knew that I am a female, let alone a queen. I just wanted to have a good fight."

He says, "I would have been among those to refuse to fight. I was raised not to harm any female. Please get up."

I obey. We take a walk together. I know he has questions. He asks, "Why deceive everyone?"

Sighing I reply, "I wanted fights. I am so good my people refuse to fight me. You are the only one to defeat me."

He asks, "How did you get so good?"

I reply, "I trained often."

He asks, "Why did your parents let you learn fighting?"

I say, "They encouraged it because they saw an older male go after a child when I was a baby and wanted to make sure that no one would be able to harm me for my wealth and gender."

We talk for hours. He is nice as a friend. I do not mention that because I bowed to him, I must obey him. I do not want to tell him. As it gets close to lunchtime, I say, "We should join my parents and sisters for lunch."

He says, "Alright. How is it that you rule when your parents and grandma are alive?"

I reply, "They are all named Monax. It was grandpa's name as well. Days after my birth, grandpa took my nickname and officially made it my last name, named me his heir as my dad did not want to rule and changed the nation's name to match my last name so only I could rule after him. I gained the throne when I turned ten."

We enter the throne room where my family is gathered. I see a couple of strangers. They appear related to my new friend. His parents. His father states, "I thought you came here to test your strength not to have a date."

I feel myself blushing at his assumption that we have dated. Then anger soars. I snap, "Your son did fight! He was the only one to defeat the strongest fighter in my land. What I do is not your concern!"

Leaving the room, I slam the door on my way out. A date! Can a female not get to know a male as a friend? I feel my guards shocked and concerned about my response and realize that I over reacted. I stand there calming down listening to the conversation. I hear my friend say, "We just took a walk this morning. The fighting ended only yesterday. I am not sure why she got so angry at your assumption. I see how you could assume what you did."

Even he questions my actions. What did I do wrong? Main stone asks, "Is he someone you are interested in child?"

No. I am not into him. I am just friends. I would consider a treaty with his family, but not marriage. Who would I marry? I do not know yet. I want love, strength, kindness, compassion and desire. I will find my forever love someday. Calm now I go back in. I say, "I am sorry that I yelled. Please forgive me. I am not used to others assuming things about me. I do not care to be embarrassed."

He says, "At least you do not object to going on a date with me."

Trying not to smile, as I would not mind dating and finding out if he has all the qualities I want, I ask, "What makes you think that?"

He answers, "You admitting to being embarrassed, and the fact that you are trying not to smile."

Not realizing he picked up on my trying not to smile until now, I gasp, "Oh!"

I turn to walk out. He grabs me, turns me to face him and kisses me. My eyes water and I shove him before I flee to the hidden library. I am sad that he forced our union and that I have to wait for many years to even date. I wish he had asked. I curl into a lounge chair in the library blinking away my tears to not hurt my people. Had he asked, I would have explained the law and why I would not allow anyone to do so. Main stone chimes, "Save his life. Let him be yours. He lost the chance at immortality because he took liberties."

Still trying not to cry, that brings fresh pain to me. I silently wonder, "Is there no way to break the union?"

Main stone says, "His death. If you cause a death, you lose me."

I question, "What about his parents' nation and this nation?"

Main stone says, "You child have two genetic lines. Your birth family's genetics would only pass to your children from the one you choose. The other genetics is Ann's and Matt's. You carry their mixed genetic code as well, just incase something happened and to give this nation an heir. That would allow you to give his home nation and this nation heirs yet not be their mother. They would be Ann's and Matt's grandchildren. The fool is trying to calm your guards down so he can come apologize. It will take him a bit. Zeffron is coming to talk."

I get up and pace a bit to get rid of the stress, anger and frustration. As I calm, the tears dry. Besides, I need to be ready to greet my sisters as they will come since it is our birthday. Zeffron shows up saying, "Calm down Sam. He is not harmed, nor will he be. I tested him before he got to this nation. He is approved of. No, I do not agree with his taking such rights, but if he has no problem with your magic, I will not punish him for doing so."

Sad, I smile saying, "Thank you. I have learned to care for him."

That is true. I have learned to care for him, just not as deep as should be for a marriage. It is only caring about life and a friend. I sit and read. My sisters enter the library. Seeing Zeffron, they all salute. They have relaxed with me as I have called them sisters all the time. Zeffron says, "Sam, your mother is explaining to your guests that you are a king. You need to go explain the laws you fall under to the fool prince."

Sighing, I set the book down saying, "Come on sisters. I need you near."

They follow me. We enter the throne room together. We are in time to hear mom say, "Sam is not married, nor is *she* less than their king. We have no gender differences in our names, titles and ranks here. The one born to the throne rules here."

As an immortal I cannot just ignore the lie she knowingly spoke. In magic common I say, "I know that mother has not forgotten the law that states 'a couple is married with the first kiss' so you deliberately left it out. Why?"

Also, in magic common mom asks, "Do you think that they would accept it? They are having trouble accepting that you are a *king*."

Where everyone can understand, I reply, "You are right, but law is what it is. It is his decision."

Going over to him, I continue, "My sisters will explain the law I mentioned. Find me when you decide."

I walk out sad as I know I will lose another life for lies break the ability to get immortality. I know my sisters will explain the law for I had said they would. I go to the magic library, leaving the door open slightly so he can join me when he decides what he wants. Minutes pass by before the prince comes in. He asks, "Sam, are we married?"

Not wanting him, I decide to give him the choice, so I reply, "We are if you are fine with who I am."

My voice drops to a whisper as I continue, "And what I am."

He asks, "What does that mean?"

Knowing better than to let his parents learn of my magic, I say, "Library lock."

Instantly the library door closes, my symbol appears on it then the symbol and door vanish. I see his shock that it did. I show him all the magic those here know of. Then I retake my outsider appearance. I say, "There are laws all magics abide by. As a magic I must obey those laws. I will show you my lands if you decide to accept those laws and me. If you cannot, I am sorry but for my people's safety I would give you a medicine to erase your memories of meeting me and what I can do, who I am. Anything that would put them in any danger."

After I tell him the magic common laws, he says, "I need time to think."

I say, "I will give you twenty-four hours. Pass that, it is a rejection and I would have to give you the memory mix to protect my people."

He nods and leaves. I am glad I only have to wait a day to know if he frees me or not. I would still have to serve him the rest of his life, but I think I could ask someone else to take that responsibility if needed and reward them greatly for it. Main stone chimes, "You could. The more that one suffered for your mistake though, the greater you would end up rewarding that one."

I turn invisible and follow him to the throne room. On our entering, his father asks, "Did you find her?"

He nods. His father asks, "So?"

My friend shrugs as he answers, "I am thinking."

Dinner is served. Then they are shown to rooms. I go to mine where a meal is waiting for me. After eating, I go sit in the library waiting for his decision. Just before lunch he enters. His decision is made. I do not have to wait long as he says, "Sam, I want you as my wife."

Heavy hearted, I place my hand in his. We go to the throne room together. On seeing us hold hands, my sisters say, "An acceptance of our laws cannot be changed."

They are right. I wish I could change it, but the law was put into place to protect many, so I cannot change it for just me. I look at my sisters saying, "Dismissed."

They leave knowing I have to adjust to this alone. My friend says, "You said you would show me your lands."

I did promise that. I seriously wish I could just pretend to die right now, but there must be heirs to the nations. I say, "Ok, let us go get my pets. They are in the stables."

We go outside. His parents and mine following. I have him stop ten feet from the stables and go in alone. Hugging my unicorns, I whisper, "Be nice to him Pegasus. We are friends."

Una asks, "Friends? His sent is near you."

I say, "Laws Una. He kissed me. I must give heirs to nations or I would pretend to die."

Una says, "We will not share that you would rather die then to be forcefully married to another."

Pegasus says, "If you had not ordered me to be nice to him, I would not let him ride me. That is what you are asking, is it not?"

Sighing, I say, "Yes, Pegasus, it is."

I lead them out to everyone. As I approach the group, I say, "These are Una and Pegasus. I ride Una. You can ride Pegasus."

With that I get on Una. My friend's father asks, "Why do you ride as a male?"

Knowing that sitting as most females' ride would unfavorably pinch my unicorn's wings, I say, "My horses would throw off anyone that sits any other way. It hurts them."

My friend gets on Pegasus. I make short sharp whistles, commanding Una and Pegasus to move off fast from the outsiders, before spreading out their wings and flying to the dragon nation. My unicorns obey, running in circles around the castle to avoid his parents then I lean forward reducing wind resistance. When alone, my unicorns spread their wings and in moments we are in the sky past human sight. After landing, I give my friend a quick tour of Diana's land. In Dragonic Diana asks, "Would you have chosen him?"

I say, "We will never know."

Diana says, "I will not obey him. I have no respect for one who takes liberties."

I nod saying, "I will not ask you to."

From there we ride my unicorns off a bit before I take us to the crystal world. Orvalina also refuses to obey him saying she does not respect him and never will. After that, I take him to the mer nation. Mertha says, "If I see him in the sea without you, I will hurt him for taking liberties with my king."

From there we ride back to my nation. On the way I dry our clothes, so no one knows we went for a swim fully dressed. I say, "Not many know of those places. Do not share. I will be letting my nation know of our marriage soon. The capital needs to see the wedding event to accept it, so until the event happens, we will not be in the same room alone together. I will set it up as soon as I can."

He says, "Aright. I only wanted to stop you from leaving. I should have asked if you would date me."

I say, "I might have. It no longer matters. I could not even date anyone else until thirty years after you die. I do not wish you to."

He asks, "What if you die?"

I reply, "Same. Also, if we have children, neither of us could remarry."

He says, "I am sorry, Sam. I did not mean to take a chance at happiness from you."

I sigh, "I forgive you. I do not forget though."

He understands. We fly back into the castle grounds as no one saw us leave, so no one should see us come back. After I teach him to care for Pegasus, we go into the throne room. His father asks, "Where did you both go? What happened?"

Neither of us answer. His dad says, "Answer me or you are no longer my son!"

My friend says, "I have nothing to say."

His father storms out. His mother sadly follows. I make the wedding ceremony preparations and the event is a week later. The capital witnesses the ceremony. That night, I in pain let him into my quarters. He asks, "Do you want to be together or wait?"

I reply, "There is no point in staying apart. We are married."

Freedom

A month later, I know I am acting as a carrying host for two nations' heirs. I go to see his mother. No one sees me. I do not want anyone to know I am there except for her. I follow her hidden until she is alone. Then I drop the invisibility. She gasps and stumbles back startled. I say, "Queen, please forgive me for startling you. I had to make sure no one else knows about my being here. I am magic and with child. One child has no magic and therefor can't live in magic controlled lands. It would be near certain death of the child to have it so, as the child would be assumed to be magic and could not defend self as such."

She asks, "Why are you telling me?"

I reply, "Because it is magic law that no nation should be left without an heir to the throne, from marriage to a magic. Your husband would not accept any children I give birth to. However, I can use my magic to transfer the child to you. You would have to be willing to do this and raise the child as your own. Also, keep the child away from magics as much as possible."

She says, "I am willing. Why keep this child away from magic?"

I say, "Until the child turns ten, the child could gain magic. If that happens, he would be a threat to the safety of the magic nations I rule and would be killed to protect the people. I have no control over that."

She says, "Oh. What else should I expect?"

I answer, "You can expect that you will be a lot more tired than usual over the next few days to weeks. It is normal. Also, you should be with your husband as soon as you can to help avoid questions about who the child is."

She agrees to do this. I touch her thinking of the male child I hold and her. The main stone teaches me how to transfer the child. Then I turn invisible again and leave. I get into a forest area and completely alone before I realize I am too tired to continue home. I stop and rest. Main stone says, "You will get stronger in time. Rest an hour then go home. You cannot stay away for long if the girl is to be accepted by even the magics."

I sigh and obey. It takes me a bit to get home as I tire easily. When I get home, my friend asks, "Where were you my Sam? You have been away for a month."

Knowing I cannot tell him what occurred, and that it is magic concerns to make sure no nation is left without an heir I reply, "Magic business."

Two months later, Matt dies. It saddens me to lose yet another life. I walk the castle for days, adjusting to that pain. Another three months then Ann dies. I hurt even knowing she would. Also, I lost help I will need. I wonder how I can do this. How can I stand up to so much death? I go sit in the magic library. Zeffron comes asking, "Why is losing your mom causing you so much more sadness then losing your dad, Sam?"

I reply, "Mother could have helped me with my baby."

Zeffron says, "Your sisters can as well."

I nod knowing they could. I just hate losing lives. Before Zeffron leaves I ask, "Do you think I can hide the baby away from me?"

Zeffron says, "It is probably safer for you to do so."

I ask, "Do you think it would be good to place her among slaves? When the child returns, she could buy those that raised her, letting them earn freedom."

Zeffron replies, "It is fine as long as they are free before the child reenters the magic controlled lands."

I knew it would be but had to ask to make sure Zeffron does not learn how much I know. He cannot learn my rank yet. I will not fail if I can prevent it. Another two months and I am having nightmares about my friend gaining immortality and our marriage becoming a forever thing. It hurts to think of being trapped forever and it hurts to think of another death. I whimper in pain. My friend asks, "What is wrong Sam? Why are you whimpering?"

How could I answer that? What could be said? I stay quiet as nothing will make this right. He leaves. Two days later, he returns with Mertha. Mertha sits by me and rubbing our mermaid marks together asks, "King Sam, show me what is wrong."

I show her that I am close to having a daughter and the nightmares I have been having. Mertha asks, "Please leave me and my sister alone to talk."

He leaves. Moments later, I give birth to a girl who looks are mine. That hurts also. Main stone chimes, "I had to make them so as that is the only way the magics will accept her one day."

I say softly, "Mertha, hide Samantha among slaves because no one would expect that a princess would live with slaves and that makes it the safest for her. Please do not tell anyone about her. I will sometime."

Mertha hides Samantha from sight and walks out. I hear her tell my friend that I would be fine, I was just having bad dreams. I quietly ask main stone what to do now. It tells me to let my friend know he had a daughter give him a few more months then I could pretend to die and it would hide me from all mortals while I wait for a while so the union will break and when it does, I can return as one of my own descendants and pick up where I left off with more magic able to be used. I think that is fine by me. Main stone also says, "If you want, I can show you what Samantha and her descendants go through."

I think I want to know. Main stone says, "Very well then. Just know your timing on months is still close to outsiders timing while I am set in the Emperor's timing. It might not seem as months to you."

As my friend has joined me, I do not sigh though I want to. My friend asks, "You were having nightmares?"

I say, "Yes. I do not want to share them with you. I have exciting news though."

He asks, "What is that?"

I say, "You have a daughter."

He seems confused for a second then asks, "You are pregnant?"

I say, "No. I had Mertha hide your daughter so the girl will stay safe."

He asks, "You just gave birth?"

I say, "A girl. Magics have children differently than nonmagics. She will rule here one day."

He asks, "What is her name?"

I reply, "Samantha."

He is pleased. The next day, we are riding away from the capital for a bit just to relax, when Pegasus darts in front of me. I hear my friend scream then see him drop to the ground with an arrow through his chest. He says, "Leave me Sam. I could not stand to see you hurt. Let me die. Thank you for Samantha."

I call out for my unicorns to leave then issue the guard inspection of the area at the nearest guard station. They find the shooter and I banish him from my nation. Main stone says, "His death starts tomorrow. Thirty years after that you are free. Do you want to pretend to die from grief or continue here?"

Not able to grieve deeply enough to fool others into thinking I died from it I chose to continue living. I go home, announce his death, let the nation morn for him and just do the bare minimum that I have to for the nation to stay strong. After a bit I learn it is easier to just keep this way than to try to pretend to adjust and get happy again. I am happy my life with him is over. Now I just have to wait out the time. I go sit in the magic library putting a do not disturb unless necessary note on the door. I spend many days here. In the many times alone, I watch as Samantha grows up as a slave. She obeys the couple raising her. Sometimes I see that she deserves punishment, yet the man raising her always takes the beating. Samantha apologies to him every time it occurs. I see that nation is prospering.

A princess raised as a slave

Samantha is no trouble to the couple minus the occasional beating the man takes to protect her though he does not know she is a princess. I see her carve the three magic symbols that she was born with onto the couple's door frame. As they come in from slave work each day, Samantha touches the symbol whispering, "Please be good to this family and nation."

The couple ask, "What is that symbol you placed there Samantha?"

Samantha replies, "It is a symbol of friendship."

They accept it. The next day, the man goes to touch it as he comes in. Samantha feet behind him yells, "No Sir, you must not!"

He asks, "Why?"

Samantha replies, "I should be the only one to touch the symbols I drew."

The couple ask, "Why?"

Samantha answers, "Please, just accept what I say."

Nothing else is said about it. I have to take care of some state business, so I do then I go back to the magic library and continue watching Samantha. Nothing noticeable happens for two years. Then a stranger comes into the area where the slave plantation is. He sees Samantha and I hate his look. It is the same look I rescued Lily from when I was days old. He touches the symbol as he was following the couple and Samantha into their home. I look away briefly as he screams. I do not look back until silence resumes. I know he burned to death from the protection curse. It still hurts to lose a life.

The couple raising Samantha gasp, "What happened?"

Samantha replies, "He touched the symbol I carved onto your door post. That is why I should be the only one to touch these symbols. They do not harm others if they are left alone."

The woman says, "That doesn't seem as friendship to me."

Samantha says, "As long as I am here and touching it regularity it is as a friend to you both."

They ask, "What if you don't touch it?"

Samantha does not answer. Instead she goes for a walk. Another couple of years pass by. The couple are always very careful not to ever touch the symbols Samantha had made. Main stone chimes, "She has been away from magic to long. Send her help."

I call Mertha and have her take Samantha the medicine to boost magic as it has been awhile since she was taken away from magics and might need it. Mertha never sees my view port. I go back to watching Samantha as soon as Mertha leaves. After a week, Samantha becomes sick. A week of her being sick and the symbol started to fade. Her promise! Oh, young one, get well before your promise breaks. Yet so far away and no idea where she is, I cannot help her. I hope Mertha arrives in time.

A princess finds her prince

A few hours later, I see a young male in prince's attire ride onto the plantation where Samantha is. He asks the slave owner, "Why has production gone down?"

The slave owner replies, "I do not know young sire. We are doing everything the same, yet not as much grows. A couple of the slaves seem worried and I have not seen their daughter for a bit, but I do not know if that is related. I doubt it."

His prince asks where and is led to the cottage the couple live in. On his way in, he touches the symbol. Panic crosses the faces of the couple raising Samantha. I know he only wants to help, so the curse will only make him mildly sick for she desperately needs help. He walks over to Samantha and with the hand he touched the symbol with, he touches her. That alerts her to the promise breaking and she screams, "No!"

The woman says, "Please Sire, do not hurt her."

He says, "I do not intend to. Why did she scream?"

They reply, "We do not know sire. She has never allowed us to touch her."

He asks, "You have never touched your daughter?"

They answer, "Sir, she is not our daughter, she was brought to us at a very young age and placed in our care. We do not know who her parents are, we never met them and the one that brought her to us said that she was just a family friend."

He notices Samantha muttering so leans closer. She is saying, "Guardians, I have broken a promise. Forgive me for that I could not prevent. Send me help."

I say, "No punishment for your being ill. It is forgiven. Correct it."

The prince sits up saying, "She says she has broken a promise and could not prevent doing so. She asks for help. Do you know what she means?"

They reply, "No, we have no idea what that means."

At that moment, Mertha walks in. She goes over to the woman and says, "You are not held at fault for this."

The woman says, "You brought Samantha to us."

Mertha says, "The highest honor I got from her mother is the protection of her child."

Going over to Samantha, Mertha sits by her saying, "Friend, I am here."

Samantha looked towards her then touched her eyes. Mertha understanding that Samantha's eyesight is off places a small container in Samantha's hand saying, "It is temporary, sit up and drink this."

Obeying the suggestion, Samantha asked, "Do the guardians hold it against me?"

Mertha says, "I hope not. You were to ill to even move. How can it be your fault? Relax. If they do not punish you within a week, I say they do not hold it against you. I am sure they know how sick you were."

Samantha says, "I hope so."

The prince asks, "What is going on?"

Samantha looks at him then noticing her symbol on his hand asks, "Why does it matter to you?"

He replies, "The land's prosperity has went down, so far the only thing different that I have been told of was you."

Samantha looks away. The couple raising her say, "Surly you do not think that she is the reason?"

Shivering, Samantha says, "Close the door on your way out Mertha."

Mertha says, "As you ask."

She leaves closing the door behind her. Samantha sighs, "Madam you don't need to protect me anymore. I am cold from fear. I am afraid as I am the reason the prosperity has went down as I divert the energy that should go into a land when I am not well."

The prince asked, "Do you understand that you just claimed to be magic?"

Samantha replies, "Yes, I am magic."

Pointing to the mark on his hand Samantha says, "That is a permanent mark though it will vanish as I get stronger it will always be there. It serves as a treaty between us. The land you and your decedents claim as home will prosper as long as I am safe. That is the treaty and I will abide by it. If you harm me, have me harmed, or allow me to be harmed when you can prevent it; it will be as a broken treaty. The symbol will change to a curse if you break the treaty made and the prosperity will severely decrease."

I hear Zeffron grant that request so she will not be assumed to be lying. The prince agrees to not harm her or allow her to be harmed. He asks, "How did I make this treaty?"

Samantha answers, "You did so by touching the symbol then touching me."

Just then the king of that nation bursts in demanding to know, "What is going on here?"

The prince replies, "I am visiting a friend."

Samantha smiles, stands, walks over to the king and without showing him any respect says, "Your son is very kind to me. Excuse me I need to take care of some things."

She walks out. The king reaches to toss her back where she would have landed on her back, but the couple and his son say, "I would not recommend that."

The woman continues, "I saw someone try to grab her once. Within moments she had that one knocked to the ground and her foot was on his neck. He never tried to touch her again. She could have hurt him bad had she wanted to."

I see Samantha go to the slave owner. He asks, "What do you want disobedient young one?"

Samantha says, "I want the deeds to myself and the couple that raised me. How much?"

He says, "You are a slave. There is no way you can afford it legally."

Samantha says, "I was born free. I keep the laws of the nation where I was born therefore, I am free. How much?"

He says, "You are lying."

Zeffron joins them, walking in to fool the human. Zeffron in male appearance says, "She did not lie to you sir. How are you Princess Samantha?"

Samantha says, "Be better after I get the deeds to myself and the couple that raised me."

Zeffron says, "Let me buy them for you Princess."

Samantha says, "How could I allow you to buy something for me when I have enough. Deeds now!"

The slave owner caves on the chance they tell the truth and tells her how much it would cost. She hands over the money and gets the deeds. Zeffron follows her out until they are past the slave owner's sight then leaves her. Samantha goes back to the cottage she was raised in. Samantha moves past the king without so much as acknowledging him. Going over to the prince, she hands him the documents to the couple saying, "These are for you."

He asks, "What is this for?"

Looking away, Samantha says, "Repayment of debt."

He seems to wonder about that but does not ask. Instead he opens the scrolls and reads them. Looking to the couple that raised her, he asks, "Them?"

Samantha nods whispering so low that I figure he verily hears her, "They are to travel with me if I leave a place and not to return. It is part of the agreement that was made with them."

He responds, "Sure. So why hand these to me?"

Samantha says, "Where they go so do I."

Buying deeds at a high cost

That is a statement she will not leave him as long as he owns them. The king leaves. His son follows. Samantha says, "We need to follow them. The prince owns you both now and I will not leave you."

The woman says, "That was not part of the agreement that was made."

Samantha says, "I can't keep the part of the agreement that is my responsibility if you are not with me. I cannot go away from one who I owe a debt to. Therefor I had to get an ownership transfer to occur for both of you. I will have to buy both of you back as that is law where my home is."

The man who raised her asks, "How would you know what the law is there when you haven't been?"

Samantha replies, "Contacts."

The couple quickly grab their change of clothes and follow Samantha out. In minutes they have caught up to the prince and king. Minutes later they come across an injured girl. I recognize her as Rose's daughter. She is three. Instantly Samantha moves to the front of the group. In doing so, she stated she was the boss of the group. I doubt the king enjoyed that.

The girl tries to move away from the group but pauses when she sees Samantha. That proves to me she recognizes her as the child I carried. Samantha says, "You will not be harmed. Tell me about yourself."

With a glance at all the others, the girl says in magic common, "Help me get home."

Samantha thinks for a moment then asks, "Are you strong enough to travel?"

The girl shakes her head no. Samantha goes to her and picked her up. Then tells her, "Lean against me, I am safe, and will get you to your home."

Nodding, the little fairy does so falling asleep. The king asks, "You know where that girl lives? I have never seen her before."

Samantha replies, "No, I have no idea where her home is. I can find out though."

The prince whispers, "Is she as you are?"

Samantha whispers back, "No, not even similar. She is magic though. A different type then I am."

The king asks, "What are you both whispering about?"

His son says, "Nothing."

Samantha replies, "Nothing of your concern."

I can clearly tell he thinks they are interested in each other. When they reach the castle, they go into the throne room. They meet the queen. I once met her. I was in my dragon looks when she came up on me. I threatened her. She did not understand, so I changed to human and told her she would regret it if she ever harmed any magic. The queen asks, "You are Sam, are you not?"

Knowing from the way the queen spoke that it is an unpleasant memory, Samantha looks away as she replies, "The queen has met my mother."

The queen replies, "I met someone who looks a lot as you do and went by the name Sam. It was not a nice meeting. So why are you here?"

Samantha says, "Sam is my mother. I am here because to serve my king is my greatest honor. I am sorry that I bring up an unpleasant memory for you. My name is Samantha."

I am sure the queen is thinking of my dragon looks as she asks, "You take after your mother?"

Samantha replies, "Yes madam."

The queen leaves the room knowing she could not force Samantha to leave. The king asks, "Why does my wife not seem to care for you Samantha?"

Samantha answers, "It is between me and her. Excuse me please, I need to return the child to her home."

The prince says, "That is fine with me."

Glad he did not object as she could not break a promise and to stay with him would have broken the promise to the fairy, to leave without him letting her would have broken her promise to him. Sense he let her leave she could keep both promises and would return to him because of it. I see Samantha go out away from any town alone with the fairy child then asks softly, "You are a fairy, right?"

The girl replies, "I am. I rule them. Mom died giving birth to me. I gained rule immediately. For your help, I name you my heir. You are kind as your mother is."

Samantha says, "A great honor you gave me."

Then Samantha sets the girl in a flower field and goes back to the prince that owns the couple that raised her. I see her faithfully serving the prince, always doing as he asks, though she does not have to. I see them standing feet apart many times. The prosperity returned to normal. The queen got used to Samantha's presence, though was nervous around her. The king often asked the reason that his wife had issues with Samantha. Neither one would answer. After a year, a small child walks over carrying a staff. Samantha shows recognition of the child. Seeing the child, Samantha asks, "Why are you here child?"

To that the child answers, "You know."

She placed the ruler's staff down hard. Only the new fairy queen would be able to move it now. In that year, the main stone says, "To keep the progress you have made, and get the generations to go by, the girl must assume you died. All but the Ancients, kings and their spouses must assume you died, as only those that know you are who you are can know until you prove your ability to lead others."

So, I had sent Mertha there with a letter. It reads as, "Child, I am not expected to live much longer. I would love to meet you before it occurs. I want to meet the couple that raised you. Sam Peacemaker."

As the fairy child and Samantha were talking, Mertha joined them. She hands Samantha the letter saying, "Samantha, this is for you."

Samantha opens it, reads it and then tells the fairy child to go with Mertha. As she did so, Samantha took hold of the fairy staff. Now fairy magic is able to be knowingly used after I join back in. The fairy nods and follows Mertha. I know they will come here. The prince, sitting beside Samanthia notices her tears. I am keeping others from feeling her pain. The guards that serve his father are able to see them but not hear them. The prince asks, "What is wrong Samantha?"

Through her tears, Samantha replies, "My mother is dying."

Without a pause, he says, "Then go to her."

Samantha says, "I cannot. Not until I repay a debt. How much would it be to purchase the two that raised me?"

She had to have them with her now as not to would break the promise made to them and as I gave her warning, I would let her suffer for her fault. The prince says, "You can have them."

Samantha balks, "No sir, it is against the law of the land that is my home. I must purchase them at fair price. If you had bought them and didn't want to give them up what would it cost one to have them?"

He tells her. She gasps. That teaches me to never assume prices. That price is what Samantha now has to pay for the couple. Since she has no money with her and can not leave his land to get the money, she would need she takes out a dagger. One I had made and had Mertha give to her so she would be able to find her way back here. Samantha cuts some of her hair. I see him wondering why. Samantha then proceeds to weave the hair into a strange shape, occasionally breathing on it and occasionally lines on her hands would turn blue. All the while she is muttering, "A blessing to the couple I give this to as a repayment of a debt I owed. Five generations of your family's rule will prosper in as long as you and they do not harm my peoples."

The guards are unaware that her hair is regrowing or that she has magic. They do not even know she had cut her hair as she had done a small memory wipe right after. I saw it go over them. As the prince watches a glass symbol forms in Samantha's hands and her hair regrows. When the symbol is complete, they go to talk to his parents. Samantha hands it to the queen. On taking it, the queen gets burned, nearly dropping it. I know the blessing is etching her DNA into it. Samantha tels her to hand it to her husband. The queen does so not being sure why she should. The king also gets burned on touching it completing the genetic blessing. Samantha tells them, "Pass it down in your family line."

They ask, "Why?"

Samantha responds, "It is a blessing symbol from my home. As long as one of your family bloodline rules in this land, the land will prosper. I gave it to you two, because I do not see this land when I look at your son. This will fully pay the debt I owed."

The prince asks, "What about our agreement?"

Samantha replies, "Remains in effect as long as we both are alive. Give me the deeds to the couple that raised me."

He does so. She takes the woman's deed and burns it, saying, "As you were promised on agreement with my mother; even though you haven't met her; by keeping me safe all these years, you earned your freedom."

Samantha puts the male's deed in her sash saying, "Sorry sir, you were not bound in the agreement, and will have to earn your freedom."

I feel her desire that he had been put into that agreement also. The prince sounding full of desire asks, "Will you return, Samantha?"

Samantha replies, "No."

Taking out the ring I made from a pocket, Samantha hands it to him saying, "The ring contains a map to my home and is the easiest way for me to prove who I am. I do not need the map, I know the way already, and there are other ways for me to prove who I am."

The king asks, "Who are you, then?"

Looking at the prince, Samantha replies, "I am Princess Samantha Peacemaker."

I see that the couple that raised her are wondering if she really is a princess and why then if she is would she be placed with slaves. The prince smiles big as he says, "Princess, huh."

The king says, "I doubt it."

His wife says, "The one called Sam that I met was a queen."

The king asks, "You sure?"

She nods. Samantha says, "I need to go."

The prince nods saying, "I love you Samantha."

Not as you seem

Blushing Samantha turns and leads the couple out. I have to close my view port at that time as someone knocked. Mertha and little fairy enter. Mertha says, "King Sam, this girl is the highest council member for the fairies and Princess Samantha recently became their queen."

I say, "It is good. Nice to meet you."

Fairy says, "You are not as you seem."

I say, "You must mean my health. I do not expect to be with this nation much longer."

Fairy says, "I expect so."

A few weeks later, I see Samantha and the couple enter the nation. I have the council test her hard to prove she has the values fit to rule them. She passes. I am glad as that means I can successfully and safely pass this nation to her. After that she introduces the couple to me. The woman, Nellie, asks, "Why have a princess put with slaves?"

I laugh, "No one would expect it. That made it safe for her. I am glad you are back Samantha. You will rule here soon."

Samantha hugs me then whispers, "You are wiser than I could ever be."

Days later, I pass rule to her with my apparent death. Hidden from everyone I watch as Samantha successfully becomes Queen Peacemaker. Over the next year, even the council notices Samantha's sadness. Main stone chimes, "She is in love."

Diana, Mertha, Orvalina and the fairy ask, "Samantha you seem sad. Why?"

Samantha says, "I had hoped for more time with mother. I miss her."

That comes off as true, but I doubt it is all of it. Then the prince that she had given her ring to walks in. At seeing him Samantha smiles big. I realize the main stone was right, she is in love.

Mertha unable to test him as she has been in his home nation three times, has met him and was there when he learned of Samantha's magic says, "The guardians have right to test him, I withdraw."

One of Zeffron's equals says, "We already have, he passed."

In moments Samantha is giving him a hug. He kisses her. Then he asks, "Samantha, marry me?"

Samantha replies softly, "Magic marriage law is that 'a couple is married with the first kiss'."

His parents do not hear her, but he does, and he kisses her again. I guess that he figures that if she had objected, she would have slapped him the first time. So, he will have her as his wife. Samantha's people starts chanting, "We accept the union of this couple. Our Queen Samantha and her choice. He is now our king."

The prince's mother asks, "What are they saying?"

Samantha replies, "It is that they accept a marriage union between your son and me. It cannot be changed. You can tell your husband why you think so little of me. In my land I cannot be harmed."

Treaty

His mother says, "I do not care for you because you take after your mother and I know that she is a dragon. She spared my life once but told me that if I ever harmed her or her people, she would make me suffer something far worse than death. You mean your mother's land?"

The foreign king gasps, "Dragon!"

Samantha says, "My mother is dead. This land is mine now. I am more than just a dragon."

The queen nervously asks, "What else are you?"

Samantha replies, "I am also a mermaid, a crystal being and a fairy. You do not need to fear me, the agreement I made with you both became part of the law I and my people must live by. As long as I live that agreement stands. It will pass unto the next five generations automatically just as long as you both don't harm me or my peoples."

The foreign king asks, "What if one of your people is harmed by accident?"

Samantha says, "See the symbols in this room. They are the symbols that my people wear at all times. Knowing them will keep you from harming them by accident."

The king asks, "What if one of my people harm one of yours and I don't know about it?"

Samantha replies, "You would not be responsible for that. However, when you found out you should punish the one(s) that did so in equal amounts that my people suffered. Doing so will keep the treaty we made intact. Not doing so is to agree with them and break the treaty."

The king says, "If they kill one of yours, what should I do? Surely you don't expect me to kill my own people. I will not even consider that."

Samantha answers, "No, I don't expect that you would, for you are a kind king and wise, doing what is best for your nation, as I do. If one of your people should kill one of mine that one would be allowed to live but would forfeit their freedom to me and should be brought to me. I hope as much as you do that it never happens."

The king asks, "Do I get all this in writing?"

Samantha holds her hand palm up, and says in magic common, "Treaty paper write our agreement."

Paper and pen appears, and the pen writes their agreement down at a very fast speed. When it is done, she grabs the pen and signs her name/title Peacemaker and getting her ring back puts the seal on it. When that is done, she turns it around saying, "Read it and if agreeing with it all, then sign it."

The king reads through it and signs it. Samantha immediately says, "Copy, Archive."

They see it completely copy then the copy vanishes. Samantha takes the paper rolls it up and hands it to him, saying, "By our signatures, our agreement stands."

Samantha is married by a ceremony so the people would accept it to the one she loves, and his parents leaves. Five months later, Samantha goes to the fairy land and gives birth. As magics could give birth anytime from three days to nine years the fairies are not surprised, and her husband has no idea. There are two girls, one to rule the fairies; Fern, and the other, Sara Ann Marie; would one-day take her place.

The fairy child stays with the fairies. Samantha takes the other one with her and goes to a different land and hides her among humans. The family that she chose has a young girl themselves. That girl's name is Anna. I am not sure why she chose to separate the sisters. Maybe the same as Ann did with me and my sisters. I do not know why Samantha chose the family she did.

ℜext generation

Immediately I switch concern to the youngest in the family line, after all, that is where I will rejoin them to get back to being a known immortal and seeing my parents again. I see Anna and Sara grow up as close friends. Both loving to dance and would encourage each other, sometimes competing against each other, to always dance their best. Over the years they preform many times at the castle for the king and his guests. The king asking for them to do so as they are that good.

When they are seven, I see them make a keepsake box together. Sara locks it with her seal so only she can open it but allows anything to drop into the box by touching it on the top. I see Sara open it once a week and take everything out of it. The only things she leaves in it is a letter she wrote, a map to the nation she will inherit and a shield. I saw Sara inscribe something on the shield, but I did not get a clear view of it.

Sara and Anna are not always near each other, sometimes not even seeing each other for a month at a time. I follow Sara and see her meet a prince from another land. They laugh together often as friends. I see them do a friendly match once. He limped for three days after it while Sara stayed near to make sure he was alright. They had a few friends with them. One day he tells her he enjoys her friendship and wants to see her often. Sara replies, "I care also. I will visit more. There are some things I need to take care of first."

Anna's parents are concerned when Sara dissappears for long times. As I am sure they think that something might have happened to her. Them being held responsible for her safety. One day after Sara turns fifteen, she and Anna are summoned to the castle to do a performance and Sara refuses to go. Anna goes to the castle and performs by herself, telling the king that Sara is not well. Anna has no idea why Sara refused to go that time; Sara had never refused before. That is why Anna assumes that Sara is not well. Sara saw the one she loves, enter the castle with his parents and knew on seeing the queen that the queen would not care for her. They had met before.

The next month they are to put on a performance to see off the king's guests. Sara does not want to go. Anna says, "Sara, he will force a doctor if you do not go. I know how you feel about doctors. Please talk to him."

Sara replies, "Very well, Anna, as you asked, for we are sisters."

They go out and ask the messenger to tell the king that they wished to talk to him before any performance. The messenger delivered their message and came back with the reply that their request was reasonable, and to come. So, they go. When it is just the king, two guards, Sara and Anna, Sara starts to talk. She says, "Sir, I do not wish to dance for your guests. I know who they are for I saw them enter the castle. I have met them, and the queen does not care for me. If you want me to dance I will though I think it better if I do not."

He responds, "I wish you to dance. Tell me though why do you not think that the queen will care for you?"

Sara replies, "I know that she doesn't care for me. She will care for me less after our dance. The one I choose to do I call 'for love and life.' We will be ready in about fifteen minutes."

She intends to give him her life. Oh, she trusts him very much. The king and his guards leave the room to allow them time to prepare. Anna says, "I have not learned that one. How does it go?"

Sara replies, "I cannot teach you. It is only to be performed for one who is loved- romantically, or one who owns the one that is doing the dancing. You should do the introducing and do the 'hunted life'."

Anna replies, "Are you owned by another? Or are you in love? I will do the intro."

Sara does not reply. She knows that after her dance it will be both. Then they go before the king and his guests. The performance is great and the only one that does not enjoy it is the queen that Sara knows does not care for her. That queen knows that Sara has magic friends and that is why she does not care for Sara. She does not know that Sara is magic, let alone to be queen of many magics. The queen looks to think that the dance Sara had done was a bunch of flirting with her son. I guess that makes her enjoy Sara less. The queen does not know that they are already in love.

At the end of her dance Sara drops to her knees before the prince and lowers her head. She will stay there until he tells her otherwise. He has to accept or reject the gift she now offers him- her life and freedom. Anna stares. I am sure she is wondering why Sara would choose to bow to this stranger when she had never bowed to anyone, not even the king in whose land they lived.

Anna's parents comes in. They look confused and scared. Anna's mother asks, "Have we done wrong Sara that you would disgrace us so?"

They had kept the king from making her bow more than once risking their own safety to do so. There is no response. I know Sara cannot until her loves decides on if he wants the gift, she offers him. Anna then asks, "Sara, what have my parents, or I done wrong that… that… that"

Anna runs from the room crying. I know she must fear punishment for her parents and herself. The prince that Sara is bowing to then notices that Sara is crying. He turns his hands palm up as he asks, "What is wrong, Sara?"

I do not think he realizes what he just did. I doubt he understands what she was offering him. Sara replies, "Nothing is wrong."

She gets up and goes over to Anna's parents. Sara says, "You did nothing wrong and could not prevent it. It will not be held against either of you. Tell Anna that she will be able to open the keepsake box we had made together now that I will not return. Ask her to show you both to where my parents live. My mother at least needs to know what has happened. You both have been very good to me and I will remember your kindness."

I know Sara must have removed her symbol from the lock as the messenger went to the king, they were raised under just encase this occurred. Then Sara faces the king of the land saying, "Sir, neither Anna nor I will dance here again."

The king asks, "What is the reason for that?"

Sara replies, "Anna will have to show her parents to a land none of them had ever been to and I will not dance anymore as I will only do as the one I have bowed to asks of me."

The king says, "Sad to have you all leave. You can come back any time. My guests mostly enjoy the dances you and Anna do."

Her love and his parents leave. Sara follows her love much to the queens' displeasure. I open another view port to see Anna and her parents curious about the keepsakes Sara left for Anna. I see Anna open the box and take out the three items. Anna says, "Only three items. A letter, a map I have no clue about the drawings on it and a shield with a crest on it. I do not understand the words on the map. I have no idea why I would even need the shield."

Anna opens the letter and reads aloud, "*Anna, I know that as the map is written you do not understand, and that the landmarks are unfamiliar to you. The shield has a translator in it. It will make the map clear to the one who has it. However, that is not the only purpose for the shield. The symbol on it declares to those that know what it means and can read the languages inscribed on it that you, and those with you, are to be kept safe. The map and shield together with the symbol that I taught you how to draw will make you my equal. Be sure not to lose any of these items. Sara*"

Looking confused Anna says, "That does not make much since, but at least I can read it. Let us pack and go meet Sara's parents. I guess I am to have the shield out though I cannot imagine what the toy is for."

The words inscribed on the shield say, "*My sister is my equal. Keep her and her parents safe. Sara Peacemaker.*"

More known magic

I see them pack and head out. Meanwhile, in my other viewport, I see Sara following the one she loves and his parents. His mother finally gets angry. The queen yells, "Why are you following us? Did you think that I did not notice that you were flirting with my son? Go home already."

Sara answers, "I go where my king goes, to serve him is my honor. I cannot go home. As to flirting, I was not. The dance I did was a commitment dance. I am committed to serve your son."

The prince looks to have questions. The reputation of the Peacemakers has apparently gotten around for a young Northwind girl comes running over to Sara saying, "Young Peacemaker please protect me."

Sara says, "I don't know you. I will protect you though, however it will be that I have equal rights as you."

Ha! Clever. The child would not object to joining the Peacemaker's council for saving her life and leaving her the most rule. The child replies, "It is fair."

A group comes then intent on killing the child. Sara kept stepping between them and the girl. One member of the group draws a sword and tries to kill Sara. Dogging, Sara arms herself as she says, "It shall be a fight then? You against me, with one substitute each. If you win the girl goes with you."

(To which the girl gasps and tries to move away.) Sara continues, "Child stay! You agreed to let me protect you. If I win you and those with you leave without her."

The one who tried to attack her replies, "That seems reasonable. How would it be judged?"

Sara says, "A three-point knock down, who manages to knock down the other and the substitute three times each first wins."

The prince grins. I am sure he is remembering his fight with Sara and know that the fools do not know what they are in for. There is nothing friendly about how Sara looks now. Sara continues, "Also, any interference from anyone that is not a substitute is considered to be a forfeit and will cause to one they are trying to help to lose."

They both name their substitutes; he chooses another of his group and Sara chooses her love. The match begins. In minutes, Sara has defeated them both. Sara says, "I won. Leave."

Someone else in the group attacks her from behind. Sara spins around and has him pinned against a tree so fast most are not sure what happened only that he had attacked her. Sara speaks in magic common language saying, "Cursed are you. Pain you feel for hurting any of my family, friends or people for the rest of your life. You would even feel their death, yet you would live through it, every single time. Neither you or the group with you will remember meeting me or the child by morning."

Releasing the fool, she says, "You will regret it if you ever try to harm me or those under my protection again."

The group leave afraid that if they do not, they will end up dead themselves. When the prince is sure that they are out of earshot he asks, "What did you say, Sara?"

Sara replies, "Sire, please don't ask."

I know she does not want to share that information, especially in front of his parents. More so as his mother already hates her. He says, "I want to know."

Seeming annoyed, Sara says, "Do not ask."

Not knowing she cannot disobey his commands and asking three times is taken as a command he asks again, "I wish to know."

Sara sighs then replies, "I said a magic curse. He will feel any pain he puts me or those under my protection through. Also, that none in that group will remember meeting me or the child by morning."

The prince answers, "Oh, sorry I asked."

His father says, "Witch, get away from my family."

Sara says, "I am not a spell-caster. I can only use certain spells. You can't make me leave nor can you harm me."

He could not harm her because only one that she had bowed to could kill her now. It was the second effect of a magic bowing to another. North wind girl groans and moves away as Diana gets near. Sara looked at North wind girl concerned. The child complains, "To hot, it is far too hot here."

North wind girl runs off. Sara asks, "Why are you here Diadon?"

Diana says, "I need to talk to you."

Sara replies, "So talk."

Diadon glances at those Sara is with before saying, "If you are sure. The Princess Anna wishes to know why she was honored so, and when she will see you again."

Sara says, "Leave..."

Diana leaves. Sara looks in the direction the child had ran off then sighs. The prince asks, "Did I understand her meaning right; you are a princess?"

Sara nods, looks towards where the child had left again and sighs. Her love says, "You can go if you want to."

Looking at him with tears in her eyes, Sara asks, "Do you want me to return?"

Smiling he replies, "It would please me if you wanted to."

Sara sadly smiles though I am sure she is glad he wants her to return. Sara says, "It matters not what I want. I will return."

Heading North, Sara travels many days going as long as she can without food or water. After filling her needs, she heads north again. Finally, she reaches a town very far north. Someone there asks, "What brought you here to the northern most town?"

Sara replies, "I am here to visit a friend."

She goes out that night staying out of sight and traveled north again. Three hours later, a very bitter sharp cold wind came up. Soon the child she had helped is near her. The girl says, "Thank you for your help. Sorry that I ran off. I keep my promises. You are my equal. My name is Ranay. I am queen of those that race the north wind."

Cool, now I can use that magic as well when I can complete my test. Sara then returns to the prince she had bowed to. He is in his home now. He asks her, "If you hadn't bowed to me, would you stay with me?"

She tells him, "You would only know that if I am freed from the pledge I had made."

He says, "I free you."

Sara says, "I chose to bow to you. I do not want to leave you. You have earned my trust and my love."

That causes him to smile. A girl about eight came up to them and handing Sara a letter says, "Friend this is for you."

Sara opens and reads the letter. It reads, "I Serene, Queen of those that Race the South Wind freely give rule of my nation and my magic over to the one called Peacemaker."

After reading it Sara holding out her hand says, "Give."

Serene hands Sara the south wind ruler objects and yanking off the necklace she was wearing places it in Sara's hand; the chain falling to the ground. Then Serene leaves. Sara's love asks, "What just occurred?"

Sara says, "That girl was called Races the South Wind. She did a title transfer and gave me her land, losing her magic in the process. Handing me the objects gave me her land, handing me the necklace she wore gave me the magic she had. I am not sure why she did so. I do not know if her people will accept me."

His mother asks, "So your necklaces contain your magic?"

Sara replies, "No. When they are yanked off our magic is transferred into them and surrendered to whoever we hand them to. Only one of equal or greater strength can remove the necklaces unless we do so ourselves."

His mother asks, "Why don't you?"

Sara answers, "It is a fate far worse than death."

His father asks, "How so?"

Sara replies, "To lose one's magic is to be treated as a traitor from all magics. None trusting you again and having to wonder with no home. Any blessings or curses that were given are removed. If non magics find out you were magic, they would kill you, or force you to reveal other magics so those magics could be killed, or both. I don't understand why Serene would choose such."

He asks, "Serene?"

Sara replies, "Serene is her name. Races the South Wind was her title."

Mertha, Orvalina, Diadon, and Fern came. Sara saw them, went pale and says, "Mother has died then."

How could I not be aware of that event? Main stone chimes, "I kept it from you because you are not able to handle the direct knowledge right now. Her death brings you closer to being freed from the forced union. I know you are still sad about the lost life."

Mertha, Orvalina, Diadon, and Fern reply in magic common, "Yes and unless you intend that Anna should be queen then you need to come home."

Sara says, "She can't be. She does not have the strength needed. As she is no longer equal to me."

Her council asks, "What do you mean?"

Sara replies, "I am equal with Races the North Wind; I am Races the South Wind."

The council understands that she has gained two types of magic. They wonder at her for it has been such a short time, only a couple of months. They also know that unless Races the North Wind; Ranay, and a stand-in from Races the South Wind's land they would not be able to make her do anything. Diana then says using magic common language, "Queen the people are not safe unless you come home."

Sara answers, "I know."

Then Sara goes over and sits by the prince. Her people have confusion with that. They know then that Sara has bowed to him and she would not be able to leave if he ordered her to stay. They wonder if they will be safe.

Orvalina asks in the common language, "Does he love you? Do you love him?"

Sara nodded to both. The council says also in common language, "If he asks for you to marry him, we have no objections."

Afterwards they leave. Sara stands sighing. She tells him and his parents, "I am needed at home, once there however my life becomes bound to the land and I will not leave very often. When I do the times will be short, few, and far between. This is to ensure my peoples safety."

The prince asks, "Will I see you again?"

Sara tells him, "Unless you go with me, we will never see each other again. If you do go with me, we would be married upon entering my land."

He smiles saying, "That is fine with me, let us go."

Sara says, "It is not as simple as that. My council has no objections, but law dictates that at least one of your parents agree or we can't get married."

For her words it became law. I know she desperately wanted one of their approvals to make it so. His mother asks, "Why should we?"

Sara answers, "The queen is wise and kind, it is good of you to not let the preconceptions you were raised with to entirely cloud your judgment. I accept that you are trying to make a wise decision for your family and the people under your husband's command."

The king asks, "I wonder what benefit we would get out of allowing a marriage to occur?"

Sara keeps quiet. His parents discuss it between them then tell her, "We will allow a marriage to occur."

Smiling Sara thanks them. Then she shows them the way to her land. Sara and her love are married, and his parents go home. I close the view port. Main stone says, "Now we advance those skills."

After I finish that, I reopen my view port on Sara and her husband. Six months have passed. His parents have come to visit. Sara takes one look at his mother and leaves the room. Sara never disrespects others. Her love asks his parents to excuse him and follows her. Catching up with her he says, "That was rude, Sara. What is wrong?"

Sara replies, "Your mother shouldn't be here. She is putting her life and her unborn child's life in danger."

She is right, my magic had felt the presence of the child. Hers must have also. He asks, "How?"

Saving a child's life

Sara states, "Young children, under age ten, and especially unborn children are most apt to gain magic that they have no right to. The guardians of the magic lands will kill the child if magic is gained as that would make the child a threat to my life. I cannot stop it. Your mother needs to leave."

Kill, no but the child would be punished and might give up on life. Main stone chimes, "We need to prevent life loss. You are continuing your test as Sara's daughter now. First alter your looks to seven."

I do so then, I am in the castle I spent years in around a corner from them. As the main stone tells me to, I go over to them saying, "Queen it is all right, the child will serve the land."

Land is another term the magics use for ruler or the one to be ruler. I know I will be. To say this land in reference to yourself was to claim right to rule. Sara says, "You call me queen, but I do not know you."

Knowing she will draw the conclusion she needs to, I say, "My name is Sam."

Not recognizing me from my disguise, the council attacks me as they had joined us moments before I said my name. However, I remember all their movements well and easily defeat them. In doing so, I proved that I am who I claim to be. His parents come to us to find out what is wrong. Sara replies, "I know that you miss are with child. I was concerned about the child's safety."

I say, "Madam, a daughter you have, she will serve this land."

Then I walk off. Main stone says, "Good job. Now we join Sara's unborn child, a replacement for the ruler of the Southwind nation."

The nest instant, I am by that unborn baby. I am not thrilled about having to act as a baby again. Sara's love asks, "Who was that?"

Sara answers, "Her name is Sam."

He says, "So, I gathered. Who is she?"

Sara replies, "Only my family is allowed to have the name Sam that is a part of this land. I am an only child."

His parents ask, "What about Anna, isn't she your sister?"

Sara replies, "We were not born sisters, not even half-sisters."

Her love thinks out loud, "You are an only child, so was your mother, and the name Sam or Samantha is only given to the one who has right to rule...would that make that child ours? But she was seven or eight?!"

Smiling Sara says, "Magic can alter appearances even looking older or younger than we really are. She would be very strong to be able to do so already. Or she could have the very rare ability, even among magics, to be able to pass through the time/space continuum. She would be very, very strong to be able to do that, I am not sure which one she did. Sam is the one person I can't get an energy read on."

Main stone chimes, "We can do both of the time-space and space-time continuums travel. I will teach you later."

Sara's husband asks, "How old is she then?"

Shaking her head as she does not know how old I am, Sara says, "Younger than the length of our marriage, but old enough to be able to defend herself if she needed to."

His parents assume, "You two were together before being married."

Sara answers, "No. Magics can have children in as little as three days or as long as nine years."

When his parents understand that they go home. Soon after Sara places the Southwind in that nation and me among humans. I go through advanced as I can get away with again and fool everyone to thinking I am a smart and strong child. After I turn seven with the couple raising me now, I take a disguise that my grandparents do not know. I go meet their daughter, Mia. On learning my name, she begs me to allow her to serve me. I agree then say, "I want to meet your parents but not have them know it is me yet. Call me Stella when near them for now. I think I will give a girl child that name one day."

Mia says, "It is my greatest honor to serve you."

After I meet her parents, being introduced as I asked to be, we talk alone in Mia's room. I whisper, "Mia, are you completely loyal to me?"

Messages

Understanding I ask if she would obey without argument, Mia answers softly, "Yes, Sam."

I ask, "Would you deliver a message for me?"

Mia replies, "Yes. To whom and where?"

I hand Mia a scroll that Zeffron had told me to get to Sara without going there myself saying, "Hand that to the Queen Sara. Say to her, 'Honored Queen, Sam sends her greetings. She is well.' Your parents know the way there as their son, your brother married Queen Sara. If your parents ask if you know Sam, just tell them 'We have met.' Queen Sara looks different than I do as I always use a disguise near you. You will know Queen Sara by her olive toned skin and long dark hair. Be safe and deliver the message after I leave."

Mia nods. I leave an hour later. Then I open a view port and watch to see what Mia does. She waits another half hour alone before going to her parents and asking, "Might I please meet the Queen Sara?"

I see total shock on their faces. I knew they had not mentioned Sara or their son. They ask, "Do you know Sam?"

As instructed, Mia says, "We have met."

They take her to Sara. When Mia enters, she goes toward Sara and holding out the scroll says, "Honored queen, Sam sends her greetings, she is well. She asked that I hand you this."

Sara opens the scroll, reads it, sighs and asks for Anna. The council who had been there the whole time wonders about that. Mertha goes and comes back with Anna. Sara says, "Anna the event I told you about has happened. I have prepared you to take my place. You need to do so now, until Sam comes home."

I wonder what event. Anna says, "I understand. I look forward to Sam coming home."

With that Anna takes hold of the staff, goes and sat on the throne. Sara walks out. Sara's husband asks, "What happened? Why the change of power?"

Anna says, "My queen forbids me to talk about it, I will not break the promise I made."

The council has no idea why power has changed, they know that when I come home, I will be able to take my place as queen. Mia and her parents go home. Main stone says, "You do not need to know yet why the power changed. Just continue visiting Mia once a year."

Second temporary union

I obey. After I turn fourteen, I meet a male. He treats me with respect, is kind and enjoys doing things for me. I know he has a crush on me. It is in his actions. I am not ready for love yet. Main stone says, "Sam, we are not close enough to rejoining the immortals to not do a repeat of your apparent death and passing the rule to another. If you care enough about him to spend time by his side as a friend as you had to with that one male, then it is as best as you should want right now."

At least I have a choice now. I think I can handle being by him for a while. Days later, I visit Mia. I am fifteen now. I say, "Mia, I care for someone and if we are allowed to get married, I want you to be there. My wedding no matter what would take place in the Peacemaker's land."

The following year I have Mia to deliver a message for me. Mia asks, "What is the message?"

I say, "My message is 'Princess Anna, what right do you have to rule this land.' This will not be easy for you to do. The council will attack you for the message. As long as you are obeying me though you will not be harmed. There is a message for the guardians."

In magic common, I say, "Tell them that Sam is willing to lose her magic with all rights as queen to have the one she loves."

Though scared, Mia nods saying, "I will deliver the message."

Drawing a protection symbol on Mia's arm, I say, "Good. Go there as soon as I leave."

I stay the night with her family then leave. Away from them I open a view port. I see Mia tell her parents that she has a message to deliver and would return as soon as she could. They still have no idea I am Sam. Mia goes to the nation I have right in and delivers my message. Assuming Mia thinks she has more of a right then the one Sara named as temporary head of state, the council attacks Mia. I figured they might. My protection symbol activates. After a moment, the guardians that are over the mortal rulers of the magics there say, "Be still, she is right to obey Sam and will not be harmed for doing so. Did Sam tell you any message for the guardians of the land?"

Mia nods and delivers the message. The council and Anna gasp. Mia asks, "What does it mean?"

No one will tell her. Feeling someone opening their viewport to watch me, I quickly close mine and go visit my friend. As I approach his home, I can tell it is Zeffron watching me. Good thing I closed my viewport when I did. My friend is a noble. His parents have dinner ready when we enter their home. We sit down and eat together, the four of us. I know they are extremely loyal to their king. My friend asks, "Marry me Sam?"

Knowing it gives me a chance to hide again as I need too, I reply, "It is not up to me, but that I want to."

He asks, "Whose choice is it?"

I say, "It is the choice of my protectors and we will have to travel to my home and talk to them."

Saying it that way to fool Zeffron into thinking that I do not know he cannot prevent my decision. My friend's father says, "We will have to get permission from the king to leave."

I say, "I will wait for your family east of this town. Please let me know if you can go or not."

Walking out, I quietly wonder, "Main stone can we hide my viewport from Zeffron? I really want to know what is going on."

Main stone says, "Girl the only ones we cannot hide from are the Emperor's family."

I open my viewport. I watch my friend and his parents go to the king of the land they live in. My friend's father asks, "Might we have permission to leave? Our son wants to marry and the one he asked does not live here. We wish to travel to her home and meet her family."

Their king says, "Alright. Check in when you get back."

I close my viewport. Ten minutes later, they join me asking, "Do we have time to pack? How far away is your home from here?"

Understanding their questions, I reply, "Pack what is important to you. My home is a bit from here. I mean it, if you value it, bring it with you."

My friend asks, "Why?"

I reply, "Not many willingly leave the nation I call home after visiting it. If they do, they are only visiting other places."

They go home and come back just after breakfast time the next morning. I ask, "Got everything you want to keep?"

My friend and his parents agree. We travel for three months before reaching my nation. I lead them into the throne room. No one recognizes me. I go to the center of the room and face the throne. I sit and wait though I feel the ruler's items pulse in recognition of my energy. They are after all items I made with my energy. They are and always will be mine. I know Mia will be here soon. I had contacted her to let her know to be here. Minutes later Mia and her parents come in. Mia seeing me seated, sits as well. The low-level guardians show up. One says, "Sam, it is good to have you home. Did you mean the message you sent to us?"

Now that Mia's parents know I am Sam, I pretend to scrub makeup off my face as I drop my disguise. I reply, "Yes, I was completely serious, my protectors. I realize that the safety of the people is your top concern."

I have to address them so for now, so I do not fail my test. That and Zeffron is watching me again. The low-level immortals say, "We tested him shortly after you two met, and he passed. Did you realize that?"

Slightly shocked they would test an acquaintance; I smile that I can go through with what I must. At least I am by someone that I chose this time. I get up and go hug the one that spoke asking the main stone to make me feel mortal as I approach her. I make it brief as the main stone says, "My presence can hurt others Sam."

After giving her the brief hug, I walk over to Anna and grab the staff she holds not using magic as my friend's parents have no idea that I have magic. After that I go over to my friend and say, "I would be your wife. Your parents can live in this land if they want to."

My friend asks, "Isn't that for the king to decide?"

Everyone laughs. Mia says, "Sir, we do not intend to be rude. Do you not know that Sam rules here? She has been Queen sense age eight."

I sigh, "I had not mentioned that fact."

My friend stares at me shocked as he mutters, "I fell in love with a royal..."

I say, "Mia, a message."

Mia gets up and comes over to me. I whisper in her ear, "Go to the nation where they had lived. Go directly to the king there and tell him that your mistress says that his servants will not return to his nation. After you deliver the message return to me."

Her eyes go wide. I feel fear radiating from her. Then after a moment Mia nods and walks out. Her parents ask, "Why did Mia seam afraid?"

I reply, "Mia is very afraid and has good reason to be. She will be safe as was the agreement that had been made."

Mia's father asks, "What agreement?"

I answer, "The agreement that was made before her birth, as long as she is in service to me, she cannot be harmed. If she breaks the agreement, she will suffer much. My mother knew that there was nothing that could be done about that and that is the reason she did not want to have your wife here when she was carrying Mia."

Only said mother as I am sill with the mortals and therefore have to. Mia's father asks, "You mean that she can't have a choice?"

I reply, "It is always her choice, she just would void the protection I placed on her years ago. That protection keeps her safe no matter the message she is asked to deliver. Take the message I just asked her to give, you saw how frightened she was, yet she did as I asked. Doing so ensured that she would be safe. My people will not let her be harmed."

Mia's mother asks very softly, "Why would they care?"

I answer, "To honor me and the promise I made. They respect me and the peace they have under the leadership my ancestors brought."

Suddenly, I feel the dewdrop ruler here. I know her name is Dewmist, but I cannot give away that I know. In magic common, I ask, "Who are you and why are you here?"

Looking confused, my friend asks, "Who is she talking to?"

The council asks, "Do you understand about the symbols of the land?"

My friend nods and I see the confusion leave his face. His parents ask, "What kind of explanation is that?"

The council says, "It is up to our queen if she tells you about the symbols, we will not."

His father notices he does not look confused anymore so asks, "Son, you know what they mean, about the symbols?"

My friend replies, "Yes. I will not talk about it though."

Mia comes in then with the king my friend's family had been raised under. The king is holding her roughly, demanding that she point out the queen she serves. The room is quiet, and he gets no answer. Mia's father utters that it did not look like she was safe to him. At that, I can no longer be still, I draw out my sword (not the katana but a different sword). I say, "Let go of my family or be killed."

Main stone snaps, "Sam! That is punishment!"

At my words all the council and the human guards in the room draw their weapons also.

That king releases Mia saying, "Tell me what is met that I lost those that had served me."

I answer, "Mia, come here."

After that is obeyed, I continue, "I have given them the option to live in this land. I expect that they have decided to. Be glad that I had a message sent to you. I could have not done so. If you ever harm my family or people, it would be the worst mistake you could make."

With that I put away my sword. The council and people follow my example. The king calms down, apologizes and says, "It really upset me to find out that I lost some of my best servants."

I reply, "I am sorry also. I should not have threatened you. I understand your being upset as they were among those you trusted the most. If they would leave so easily then how can you be sure others do not feel the same."

He nods. I continue, "Sir it is not that there is anything against you. Quite opposite they have high respect for you. It was not an easy choice for them to make."

At that he asks, "Why do they wish to leave then if they have nothing against me?"

I reply, "For their son's happiness. He is to be my husband."

Thinking I know I have to apologize deeper for my wrong. I decide to give him and his wife a child, but I would send the medicine to his wife as he threatened Mia. I ask my council in magic common, "Does my council think it would be right to gift his wife and him a child?"

They agree. I go back to where everyone can understand saying, "My advisers agree with me that it would be unwise to have them leave your land without giving something in return. My gift shall go to your wife, and Mia will bring it soon. Please leave now."

He does. Mia wonders, "Sam, why have me go back there: He was so angry."

I wait, giving him time to get out of my castle before answering her. I say, "His wife is not at fault for that. That is the reason that she will receive the gift and not him though it benefits them both."

Then I take a small sharp stone and wrap it in a cloth, keeping everyone from seeing it. I silently put a spell on it to give the lady whatever she wants the most on her asking for it. Handing the stone wrapped up to Mia, I say, "Take this to his wife, wait on handing it to her until it is just you and her and say 'My queen honors the queen of this land with a gift, though they have not met.' Place it in her hand and then ask her what it is that she wants the most of anything. When you have completed this task for me you will have completed your part of our agreement and will not have to deliver messages anymore."

Mia hugs me tightly then runs out excited. I figure she is in love to react that way. Laughing I say, "It might not be so easy to get to be alone with the queen of that land. The king is sure to let his guards know to look out for her and warn him if they see her. I am serious though, when she is done, she will be done delivering messages for me and then can get married."

Punishment again

Mia's parents smiling say, "We thought that she might have to serve you until she died and left no heir to the throne."

Main stone says, "Punishment time. No control do you have."

I find myself unable to prevent saying, "An heir she will have, a son, and that boy will not inherit that which she would not have had if she had not been exposed to it at far to young an age. That will keep him free from the trouble she went through."

Mia's father asks, "You mean my daughter has magic?"

I wince. The main stone still has control over me. It uses me to ask, "Did I say that?"

Knowing it will not be nice when this is done. I look away. Mia's father says, "It was implied."

Main stone uses my voice to ask, "Was it?"

Then it tells me, "Now you have control again."

At the same moment, I hear the low-level guardians behind me yell, "SAM!"

Everyone faces them. I sit giving them authority to correct me as is necessary. My council salutes. One of the low-level guardians says, "Do not lie. We will punish you harshly if you do. Humans fear us enough, without having reason not to trust us."

Gasping from their assuming I would lie, I nod and say, "The guardians are wise and fair I accept their judgment."

My friend says, "You're crying, please tell me why."

That hurts as I know those under my command can feel it. Main stone says, "No Sam, I would not let them all suffer so. You have not broken laws. Got very close to doing so, but you are just a child still. He is expecting an answer."

Unwilling to share I say, "I will not talk about it."

I get up and walk out. I stand outside of the throne room just calming myself. I hear my friend ask, "What occurred? What did they say to make her cry?"

My council replies, "We did not understand."

His parents ask, "Is your girlfriend a witch?"

A moment later, his father asks "Why do you not answer the question? It is simple."

I know my friend might be having trouble answering that as he knows of my magic, so I quietly go back in. I speak up saying, "Questions about my ancestry should be asked to me. If you are asking if I am magic then yes, I am, but I am not a spell-caster. I did not wish you to know because it would change your opinion of me. The symbols in this room represent the different types of magic that I am."

Again, saying it as I must to keep my mortal disguise, so I can pass my test. The spell caster abilities are not known about yet. My friend's father looks around then says, "I count six, name them."

I answer, "Mermaid, Dragon, Crystals, Fairy, North-wind, and South-wind..."

Then knowing I will place the child I will pass rule to in that nation I add, "Elf."

My friend's father says, "That is seven; you said that 'the symbols in this room represent the different types of magic that you are' so why are there six symbols and you named seven things?"

I answer, "I do not have elf magic, it is not a part of this land. I included it as I see a treaty, in time/space, within five years."

The council gasps, "You can time travel!"

I say, "Yes, I have done it all my life."

As far as they know it might have been a gift from a poem to me because of their last queen. She would never tell them, and I will not say either way. My friend looks shocked. I have promised never to use my magic against him, so I do not know what is going on. I trust him with the knowledge of my magic, but the look is stressing me. I ask, "Is something wrong?"

My friend says, "I just realized that I do not know what all you could do."

Elves

I sigh, "If you need to know then I would tell you, it is safer for you if you do not know everything."

The marriage ceremony happens a month later. Two months after that, I have the main stone hide my presence from everyone and go into the elf lands. There I find a couple. I go over to them asking, "Will you raise this girl for me?"

They agree asking, "Who are you?"

I say, "You will learn in time."

Then I place the girl I named Stella into the woman elf's hands. I quickly leave after doing so. I go home and gift my friend and his parents, knowledge of magic common language. Three years later, a small elf boy comes in as the four of us are eating. I recognize the high-ranking elf council member though he does not know me. Elf says, "Peacemaker, my king asks for a treaty with your lands. He wants to know what he needs to do."

Glancing at him to analogize I heard him, and curious, I ask, "How is your king doing?"

He replies, "My king is well. What does that have to do with a treaty?"

I ignore that and write on a paper,

Sir Elfin, I think that a treaty between our lands is good. You asked what you would need to do. I have been in your land, without being known, within these past three years and know that you have a very young son, I have a girl that is about his age. I hid her in your land to keep her safe. Her safety will ensure the treaty between us.

It is my hope that our children might meet and perhaps come to love each other. They can marry whoever they want to of course, I just ask for her to be safe. If they do learn to love each other I would have no objections.

Your son is allowed to come here anytime. I look forward to meeting you and your family. I will not talk of her anymore and appreciate you not talking about her either. Best regards Sam Peacemaker

Sealing the letter, I hold it out saying, "Take it to your king."

My friend takes the paper and gives it to the elf boy. The elf leaves. Months later, I get a letter that says, "I agree to that. Plan to meet next year."

Exactly a year later, the four of us are having dinner when three strangers walked in. It is the elf king, prince and I assume the queen. Elf king says, "Pardon me, I am looking for the one called Peacemaker."

I say, "Sir Elfin, a pleasure to meet you, this must be your wife and son, nice to meet them too. I am Sam. This is my husband and his parents. Join us for dinner? Yes. Tell me more about your people."

Just doing the necessary political politeness so no one learns I know it all already. The table is instantly set for three more people from the guards in the room. Elfin and I are soon talking as old friends in magic common. Because his son is also an elf, the boy can keep up with the conversation with ease. As I gave my friend and his parents knowledge of the common language, they can keep up with the conversation decently well also.

However, I notice the one I assume is the elf queen does not join in the conversation. It gets more apparent as the meal continues. She seems very confused. Given her confusion, I doubt she knows her husband and son are magic. She probably does not understand much if anything of what is said. She must feel very alone here. It is wrong to leave her out of the conversations. I stop and go to human language saying, "I am sorry miss, you do not understand what we are talking about, do you?"

She replies, "I do not even understand what you are saying most of the time let alone the meaning. Even my son seems to know what is being talked about and I don't even recognize the language."

Does not even recognize the language! She has never even heard her husband speak it! I snap, "Elfin, do you mean to tell me that your wife does not even know who you are?"

He asks, "How is that your concern?"

Now I am mad. With my anger, a water band appears on one of my arms and a fire band on the other. I steam, "How do you expect others to trust you when you do not even trust your family?!"

I walk out. Talks will not continue until he talks with his family. I stand there waiting to see if he will. Elfin says, "I do not think she understands how hard that is."

My friend says, "How hard what is, to tell the truth. I think she knows precisely how hard it is."

Elfin asks, "How can you be so sure?"

My friend replies, "Because my parents and I all had a hard time accepting who she is."

I did not realize he had a hard time accepting me. I guess that is why I do not think of him as more than a friend. Elfin asks, "You are not...?"

My friend says, "No."

Elfin says, "I thought that you were, you seem to understand the conversation."

I guess I should explain that, so I go back in and say, "He understands because I gave him the knowledge of the language. He and his parents are more as your wife then either of us."

Elfin replies, "Oh; I had assumed that they were magic as we are."

His wife gasps, "Magic!"

My human guards heard that. I motion for stillness. They stop moving instantly. Unsure of my safety they are far more alert then moments ago. I know none of them saw me use magic. They do not pay enough attention to notice what I do. Elfin replies, "Yes love, I am magic-an elf- and so is our son. I am the king of the elves. Sam Peacemaker has a treaty with my land, she is a Mermaid, a Dragon, a Crystal, a Fairy, a North-wind, and a South-wind. We were speaking in magic common language. I am sorry for not telling you sooner. I should have."

His wife asks, "Can I meet your people the elves?"

He agrees. They leave with their son following. I ask, "Questions?"

A guard questions, "You are not afraid of them?"

I reply, "No reason to be. I am magic as well. The last Queen Monax was magic. Her son as well. His wife was a different type of magic. All called Peacemaker have had magic. Got issues with that?"

Silence. I sigh, "I use magic to protect this nation and all who call it home, our allies and help us. Do you fear me?"

He says, "Trying to adjust to information. Would you have ever told us?"

I say, "Depends on trust level. After all many nonmagics try to kill magics. Why would I want to increase my risk without trusting the one I mention it to?"

He asks, "What magic are you?"

I reply, "You heard that."

Then I go to my quarters and get some rest. Thirteen years later, I am looking in on Stella when I see Elfin and his wife get close to her. Elfin had still been doing individual introductions, but he does not recognize Stella, so he stops talking. His wife asks, "Who is the girl?"

Shaking his head, Elfin says, "She is not one of my people and I do not know her name."

Stella says, "Sire knows who I am though and why I live in your land. I will not tell you my name yet. Pardon me."

She turns to walk away when Prince Elt Elfin comes over saying, "Stella, wait up."

Stella stops. Elt asks, "Stella, do you want to go racing?"

Laughing, Stella replies, "You know that I enjoy racing. Same rules. I give you a five-minute lead."

Elt takes off running. Elfin asks, "So, your name is Stella?"

Stella does not answer that. Instead she asks, "Will you count how many times I spin in a circle before your son catches up with me?"

Elfin questions that with, "You gave him a big lead and you still think you will beat him?"

Stella nods, then as the five minutes have elapsed, she takes off running. Within moments she had caught up to Elt, they kept pace for a lap then on the third and final lap she pulls ahead. When Stella gets to Elfin and his wife, she started spinning. When Elt finally gets there out of breath, Stella stops spinning asking, "How many spins did I do?"

Elfin answers, "I counted eighteen."

Stella laughs. Elt groans, "Eighteen. You have been toying with me, haven't you?"

She laughs again saying, "It is so much fun to race you, when you are ready to try again let me know."

With that she walks off. Elfin asks, "Son, what do you know about this girl you call Stella besides, she enjoys racing?"

Elt replies, "She asked me to promise not to talk about her and I made the promise."

Well, that seems to me as if he at least respects her. They either have a treaty, or he loves her. Either way she gets elf magic which will allow me to knowingly use it again in my next part of this test for my last name. I go take care of duties around the castle then watch Stella again. She is good for the couple I placed her with. Stella and Elt race often. She always gives him a big lead then wins. He must enjoy her company to keep challenging her knowing he will probably lose. When Stella is sixteen, Elt has her over for dinner. I have watched her for a few days, and she has not ate in that time. She has not touched what they have served. Elt asks, "Is it not what you want Stella?"

She does not answer. Elt touches her sleeve whispering, "Do you see me Stella?"

Stella blinks then looking at him says, "I am sorry. Did you say something?"

Elt replies, "You are not eating."

Stella says, "Oh, I was just thinking."

Elt asks, "What about?"

Stella starts eating her food. Elt asks again, "What are you thinking about?"

Shaking her head, Stella says, "I am not answering that."

As is a yearly event, I have messengers go to each of the allies I have asking them how everyone is doing, if anything is needed and any concerns. My messenger arrives at that moment. The messenger says, "Sire, Queen Sam says that she is glad your people are well. She asks if anything is needed."

Elfin replies, "No."

The messenger sets out to return to me. I notice Stella seem to freeze at my name. She is so still that my magic barely notices her breathing still. Elt notices Stella's stillness and whispers, "Stella Ann Marie."

At that Stella blinks then says, "I am sorry. I was thinking too much again, was I not?"

Elt nods. After dinner he walks her back to the couple that raised her. At the door to their home Elt asks, "Why do you react so to that name?"

Stella asks, "What name?"

Elt replies, "You know what I am talking about."

Sighing Stella asks, "Have you ever met her?"

Elt asks, "Did she hurt you, my Stella?"

Blinking back tears, Stella says, "She would never hurt me."

Elt asks, "Then why are you crying?"

Stella replies softly, "You called me yours, and yet assumed that my mother would hurt me."

Shock registers on Elt's face. He whispers, "The great queen is your mother?"

Stella nods. The couple that raised her come outside then and notice her tears. With concern and teasing they ask, "Don't you think it is late, time to get home and get some sleep."

Elt nods asking, "See you tomorrow Stella?"

Stella goes inside. The couple comes in moments later demanding, "What did he do to make you cry? If he hurt you, or even tried to, we will take it up with his father."

Stella stops crying as she says, "He did not, cannot, and would not hurt me. Tell me about mother. I have been thinking of her and was just a little overly emotional."

They tell her, "You know that we do not know your mother, we only met her when she brought you to us asking us to keep you safe."

The next day she takes a walk with them. They come across the royal family. Elt says, "I am sorry that I upset you last night Stella."

Nodding Stella says, "I know you did not mean to."

Before his parents can object, Elt asks, "Will you all join us?"

The couple reply, "We do not want to intrude."

They start to walk off. Stella asks, "Did you mean what you said last night?"

Elt replies, "Yes, though I wouldn't have said it if I had known that it would make you cry."

Elfin and his wife immediately ask, "What are you talking about?"

Stella says, "Not all tears are bad, some are from surprise, you surprised me is all."

She starts to walk off, but Elt touches her arm saying, "My Stella, I love you."

Stella looked at him her eyes wide with happiness reflecting in them. Elfin asks, "Stella, are you Sam's daughter?"

Instantly Stella becomes super still. I wonder about that. Elt whispers, "Stella Ann Marie."

At that Stella blinks answering, "The king knows as was the letter given to him that her child was not to be talked of. Why then does he do so?"

Elfin says, "Only me and my wife knew of that letter and the contents it said, so you must be her daughter."

Stella smiles, "Sir Elfin, you are a wise and kind ruler to your people. I see their respect every day and know that mother was right to have a treaty with you. It will not be necessary to send messengers much longer. When I go home the agreement you made with her will be permanent. I have always been safe in your land, and enjoyed living here, and now have love too. I know that a messenger just got back from her land, however I want to deliver a special message. Do you mind?"

Elfin says, "It is fine with me."

He summons the messenger. When the messenger arrives, Elfin says, "Deliver the message that Stella has to Queen Sam."

Elt immediately whispers, "Stella Ann Marie."

Stella says, "Thank you Sir Elfin. My message is 'Honored queen, Stella sends her greetings. It is that what you thought and hoped that would be is. Please come visit.' Deliver my message now."

The messenger looks at Elfin and at Elfin's nod, the messenger headed off. Stella smiles. Elt asks, "What did the queen hope for?"

Stella replies, "That I would find love."

Elt asks, "Who is it that you love?"

Stella replies, "You called me yours. I truly am."

That makes Elt smile very big. Stella smiles too. Stella asks, "Do you want to race?"

Elt replies, "Sure."

The couple that I had placed Stella with, had been far enough away not to hear the conversation. Stella and Elt race, three times around the elf land. At that moment, the elf messenger comes, so I quickly close my view port. I follow the messenger back to the elf land where Stella and Elt are just finishing their race. Stella does six spins before Elt catches up. As I approach them, Elfin stands showing me respect. His wife and the rest are quick to follow. I see many elves glance at Stella then back at me. I see their understanding we are connected. Some whisper, "Think she is a guardian? What about the girl?"

Elfin says loud enough all his nation will hear it, "Queen Sam Peacemaker, it is an honor to have you here."

Elt whispers Stella's full name. Stella says, "My queen it is good to see you."

I had not expected her to be formal. Then feeling Zeffron watching me, I say, "Come now daughter no need to be so formal. Or did you not expect that I would come with the message you sent."

The ones that raised Stella now look afraid. I doubt they could be more afraid, even if they learn I am a guardian. Not as if I would ever tell them without their gaining immortality. Then only after my test is over. Stella glances at them apparently feeling their fear as well. She whispers very low, only my magic picks it up, "Mother, they fear me now."

I go over to them saying, "I had deliberately not told you that I am a queen. I knew that it would affect how you acted. I am grateful that you kept my daughter safe for me. Ask anything, I will answer your questions and I would give you a gift."

The woman asks, "Is it true that you have more than one type of magic?"

I answer, "Have you not seen my daughter use her magic?"

They shake their heads. Stella says, "I have not used any magic here except that what keeps me this size. I thought it best that no one knew how strong I am."

I say, "I see. It is fine. As to answer your question, yes, those rumors are true. I have six different magic energies, some fire, some water and some neutral."

Stella suddenly collapses. Elt catches her saying, "Stella, what is wrong?"

Noticing her do so, I move over by them and do a magic scan. No one would question that as even the mortals can do them, though not as strongly as immortals can. I keep mine at low levels. I say, "Her energy is too far out of alignment, she needs help. She needs to be taken home. The guardians can help her. You must go there to as she won't want to be without you and once there she will not leave often."

Elt says, "I do not know the way."

I wonder why he does not as he has been there. Not enough time to figure that out. I must save Stella's life. I say, "Do an ethro follow. You do that by saying it and stepping where I am as soon as I vanish. Understand?"

Elt says, "Yes sire."

I nod saying, "Ethro follow."

Then I am in my castle. I move a couple feet. Then Elt shows up holding Stella in his arms. I say, "Place her in the center of the room."

The Lights

Elt does so. The low-level guardians, those who should be enough to help her show up and do their best. I can feel it, but I cannot mention that or even try to help her myself. Stella does not wake up. Worse her energy drops again. What is going on with her? The low-level guardians say, "We do not know what is wrong with her. Sorry."

Elt looks afraid. I sit on the throne and try to prepare myself for having to hold another child. I am not prepared and do not wish to have to do so. Over the next few hours, Stella's energy keeps decreasing. At sunset, the mortal queens of the sunbeams and moonbeams show up. Sunbeam Seetha, and Moonbeam Malay say, "We can help her if you let us."

The low-level guardians give them permission to do so. I do not know if they can. They walk over to Stella and both drop their nation's royal symbol onto Stella. The symbols vanish into Stella's body. Seetha and Malay both call her Princess in their native languages. Stella's energy starts increasing. Perfect! Now I will be able to use those magics at the next phase of my test. Moments later, Stella wakes up. Seeing Seetha and Malay, Stella says, "As I promised, as I do. Thank you."

Seetha and Malay leave. Stella says, "I will be asleep for a few days as my body adjusts to the magic I just gained. I am fine, just very tired."

She yawns and goes back to sleep. The low-level guardians say, "Well, that explains why we were unable to help her. We cannot do anything against a promise made."

Elt asks, "What promise is that? Do you know?"

The guardians reply, "We have no idea."

I wish I knew, but as respect for individual privacy, I cannot learn without Stella telling me. I also could do nothing against a promise. No one could. It is a few days at dusk before Stella wakes up. Seetha and

Malay are back. Stella smiles at Elt before facing Seetha and Malay saying, "Thank you Seetha and Malay. Do your people accept me?"

They answer, "Our people trust our judgment, yes they accept you, and as queen with equal rights as such."

Stella says, "You both are very kind. I know that it was not an easy thing to do. You both are members of my council now."

With a nod, Seetha and Malay leave. Stella stands asking, "Have Elfin and his wife came yet?"

I reply, "Not yet. I expect them tomorrow."

Stella asks, "Can we be married tomorrow at dusk? Or dawn the next day?"

I reply, "After his parents get here."

Stella nods. I ask, "What promise did you make to the lights?"

She replies, "I promised them that on the day that I declared intent to be married I would fall asleep and my energy would drop until they both came to help me giving me some of their magic and rights as princess of both lands. In exchange they would be a part of my nation and safe as my people are and have access to the products my lands make. They both agreed to it. I made the promise when I was five."

I nod and thank her for sharing with me. The next day at dusk, Elfin and I both recognize Stella and Elt's marriage before my entire nation with my entire council, Seetha and Malay here. Also here is the couple that raised Stella. Then I place Stella as the new ruler here. I know I do not plan to stay where mortals know about me much longer. Also, the main stone has agreed to hide me once again. Stella faces the couple that raised her asking, "Have you decided on the gift you want, as it is now my responsibility to keep that promise."

They say, "You were a joy to have, we cannot think of anything that would equal that experience."

Space and time continuums

Smiling Stella says, "Then my gift to you is your own child." The ruling staff lights up as I grant them that for their taking Stella in when I asked them to. The woman hugs Stella saying excited, "Thank you!"

A few days later, I fool everyone into thinking I died. Once more I stay hidden as I watch through viewports what happens. Nothing noticeable happens over the next couple of years. Then I see Stella go for a walk into the Poem nation. I hide her presence from everyone she does not directly interact with. Stella hides her daughter in that nation keeping out of sight from the couple she asks to raise the girl. As she kept out of sight, I kept her energy signature hidden from them too. After hiding her girl, Stella goes visit the king of the Poems.

King Poem, male asks, "What brings you here, Queen Peacemaker? Do my people have reason to be concerned?"

Stella answers, "No reason for concern Sire. I come just to visit. I think we would both benefit from a treaty."

He replies, "I know how you would benefit; you gain a land. Tell me then how you think I would benefit from a treaty with you."

She says, "Your people would have the protection of my nations, access to the products produced, and a gift for your family from me."

He asks, "Why a gift mentioned differently?"

Stella replies, "For the safety of my child hidden in your land."

The treaty is agreed on and Stella leaves and goes home. No one even realizes she had been gone. None even know that she has a child. She has named her girl Winlight. Main stone says, "You have had enough watching them for a bit. It is time you learn space movement in the time continuum."

I obey closing my viewport. Though I follow the main stone's commands, it is hard to do. It takes me a while to master moving through space without walking or using my magic. Once I master that, main stone chimes, "That was the easy part. Now to learn moving through time in the space continuum."

Following directions, I still struggle with that. Again, it takes me a while to master this skill. When I have main stone says, "Enough lessons for a bit. You need time to recover from them. In the meantime, Samantha's descendants have passed sixteen years without your watching them. No wrong done. I just think you want to know about the ones whose family line is where you will continue your test."

I look in on Winlight, the daughter Stella hid. I see that she has learned all spells the Poems have. I accidently speak the immortal poem while watching her. She memorizes it also. I then tell her not to use it as it is not good for mortals to use. She obeys. Days later, I see her sit outside of the guardian circle for the Poems. She does not move from that spot. Days go by with her sitting there. The family raising her gets worried so asks their king to make her move. He comes to her asking, "Winlight what do you want or need?"

Winlight does not answer him. He says, "Fine but don't blame me if the guardians don't take kindly to you."

He walks off. His son also tries to get Winlight to move. Still no response. In the Poem prince's voice, I hear a far deeper caring then even the couple that raised her. I am sure he loves her. Another couple of days and the guardians directly over the poems ask, "Winlight what do you want so much that you are willing to risk your safety for?"

Winlight replies, "Might I speak to the guardians alone?"

One of them holds out a hand she gets up and places her hand on that ones. They all vanish from the mortals. My view port instantly shifts to view the area Winlight is in now. The low-level immortals demand, "Now tell us what you want."

Winlight asks, "Do the guardians know who I am?"

They reply, "We have always known, and made sure you were safe. This land does not need war with your mother. So, what is it that you want?"

Spell caster magic

Winlight replies, "I am in love with the prince. If you do not approve, then please order me to leave the land and not return. I ask for I could not bear to see him married to another. If he does not care for me have him send me away. I promise to keep the treaty that was made."

They tell her, "We would have no objections if he asks you. Leave our circle now."

She obeys. I see all Poems wonder what had happened, yet none ask. I do not think they dare. The next day I see the Poem prince take someone to dinner for a birthday celebration. While the girl is into him, he just tells her that it is his custom to be polite to others and celebrate birthdays with others. A custom he would not continue once he was engaged. The female instantly asks, "Are you interested in me?"

He replies, "No. There is no future for us. This is the last birthday dinner I will treat you to."

She is very disappointed. The evening seems to be sour for both of them after that. A week later Winlight turns seventeen. Poem prince asks, "Winlight, join me for dinner."

Winlight accepts. They watch a movie of her choice. After the movie they go to dinner. Near desert Winlight is laughing hard enough to cry. As the tears flow from happiness, it helps others, so she is not in any trouble for them. I see Prince Poem move his seat closer to her. Winlight does not notice. He does it again until he is seated next to her instead of across from her. Winlight calms a few minutes later. Once she does, he asks, "Winlight will you marry me?"

With a deep blush and high excitement, Winlight whispers, "Yes, oh yes."

He asks, "Are we telling your family first, my family first, or at the same time?"

She replies, "Yours, just because it will be the simplest."

Wondering about that, he asks, "How so?"

Winlight replies, "Because the couple that raised me are not my parents. You have never met them."

He says, "Oh, that would complicate things. When do you want to let my father and mother know?"

She shrugs, "Not today, other than that it doesn't bother me as to when."

He asks. "How about the day after tomorrow then, giving us time to enjoy our engagement."

Winlight says, "That is good, dinner then, you and your parents, me and the couple that raised me. At the castle?"

He says, "Yes."

Then he hands her the ring he has for her. Winlight tries it on. It fits. She smiles at him, takes it off and puts it in a pocket saying, "I will wear it after your parents and those who raised me know."

He nods and walks her back to where she grew up. The couple ask, "Did you have a good time?"

Winlight says, "Yes."

She walks into her room and closes the door. Prince Poem says to the couple that raised Winlight, "You both and Winlight are invited to dinner at the castle day after tomorrow."

Without letting them have time to respond, so they do not have a chance to reject, he leaves. They immediately go to her door and knock. Speaking loud enough to be sure she hears them they ask, "Did you know that he was going to invite all of us to dinner?"

Winlight replies, "I had an idea that he would."

They ask, "What about?"

She replies, "What makes you think that I would know?"

They ask, "Do you know?"

Winlight says, "I might, I might not want to talk."

They know that she will not answer any more questions at that time, so they let her sleep. The next day, they try again to find out why they had been invited to the castle. Every time they even bring up the subject, Winlight goes very quiet. By dinner they ask, "You aren't going to tell us, are you?"

She shakes her head 'no.' The next day they all go to dinner at the castle. When they are all seated and have eaten something, the king asks, "So, son why did you invite them all to dinner?"

He replies, "I am in love with Winlight, and we want to get married."

The couple who raised her say, "We can't give consent as she is not our daughter."

Winlight says, "He knows that. Perhaps it is time then that you get to meet my parents."

They ask, "How does he know? We made sure everyone thought that you were our child."

Winlight replies, "Everyone except me. I told him when he asked me to marry him, two days ago."

The king asks, "They're not your parents? Then who is? Do you know?"

Nodding Winlight says, "My mother is Stella."

King Poem asks, "Do you mean Queen Stella Peacemaker?"

Winlight nods. King Poem says, "Lets go, I do not want her mad at me."

The couple that raised her asks, "Is Winlight a princess?"

Winlight says, "I knew that you had no idea, she had kept herself in the shadows and did not tell you her name. I have always known who I am."

The six of them go to the Peacemaker's land. Stella asks, "King of the spell-casters what brings you here and with such a group?"

Her council is there and wants to know too. He answers, "Queen it is that my son plans to marry their child, except they are not her parents. She claims that you are her mother."

The council gasps. Stella says, "Good. I realized that they were the ones I had placed her with. I have no objections to their marriage."

Stella's husband comes in then. Seeing them all, he asks, "New friends?"

Everyone around the room laughs. Winlight asks, "Does Sire king not know who I am?"

Stella says, "Child, only you and I knew who you are. Only one other person even knew that I had a child and that is the spell-caster king. I only told him because I had placed you in his land and realized that you probably would end up in love with one of his people."

Winlight blushes. Her father asks, "We have a daughter?"

Stella nods saying, "I did not mention anything because the less that knew the safer she was."

He asks, "You did not trust that I would not put her in danger?"

Stella replies, "No that is not so. I did not tell you because I knew that you would be excited. I did not think that you would keep that excitement to yourself."

He asks, "Why would I?"

Stella replies, "That is my point. If the wrong person learned of her existence before she could defend herself, she would have been in danger. Remember many humans fear us magics and would kill us, a magic child they would love to kill. More so with the royal families. My family line being so strong, our child would be a top priority to kill."

He says, "You could have reminded me of that."

Winlight looks pale. I realize she is doing time travel. Main stone says, "Not just any time travel. She hit near us as we were future time traveling. That is what she is doing."

Prince Poem asks, "Winlight are you alright?"

Stella says, "She is doing time travel, do not touch her it would disrupt her magic. Does she do it often?"

The woman that raised her says, "At least once a year. When she was seven, I made the mistake of touching her while she was doing that, she came out of it fast and fighting. I could verily defend myself it happened so fast; I was sore for weeks afterwards. I never tried to touch her when she was that way again."

Her husband asks, "Is that why you both seemed leery of each other that one day and you were limping?"

She nods saying, "It hurt a lot and I did not know that I had frightened her and shut her magic down. Later, before you got home, she explained that to me and asked that I never touch her again when she looked that way. I asked if she realized that I had no intentions of getting hurt again. She cried at that and hugged me. When her tears stopped, I realized I was not as sore as I had been, and I did not look as bad as I had either."

Winlight stops time traveling then looks at her and says, "I remember that. I did not even know who had touched me. All I realized was that my magic had shut down and I was scared for my life. I reacted to that fear, I did not mean to hurt you. I would have healed you completely if I had not gotten so tired from the experience."

Stella asks, "So, you can time travel at will, and hear what is going on around you?"

Winlight nods saying, "Yes now I can. After that experience I did not want someone else I care about to get hurt so I developed the skill of knowing what was currently happening around me while in a state of time travel. It was very hard at first but has gotten much easier the more I practice."

Main stone says, "More lessons for you Sam. A mortal cannot be more skilled than you are. Especially as you have me."

Stella asks, "Where do you go when you time travel?"

Winlight says, "I am not sure. I have no memory of the places outside of my time travel and have no idea how to get there."

Water and fire magic

A gasp goes out from the council. Time travel is extremity rare to begin with even with the poem abilities. No mortal has even heard tale of one who could time travel to the future. They understand that the only way she would not know the place or how to get there was to future time travel. I silently wonder how many can do future time travel.

Main stone chimes, "Emperor, his family, their spouses, the accepted nonrelated siblings of the Emperor's children, their spouses, the Emperor's council and their spouses, those that pick up the main stone pieces off of any object the Emperor made and their spouses and those that started as poems with the shards of an immortality item along with their spouses. The only mortal that knows it that I have ran across so far is Winlight. That is all of them. It is very rare. Rarer is the ability to be in more than one time at the same time. I will teach you how when you are ready."

At that moment, in my view port I see the Water spinks queen, Aqua Marine, and the queen of the fire spinks, Felice, walk in. Turning to face them, Winlight says, "Friends, I have long waited for you to come."

They both ask, "Do I know you?"

Winlight laughs, "No, I don't think as that you do, but I know you. You both seek peace treaties with this land. Such is that I have already wrote up the treaties, expecting that you would come. Here they are. I know you find them agreeable as in times future/past we discussed them."

She hands them the treaties and laughs at their confused expressions. They open them and read. Both being surprised that they did not disagree with anything written. They both sign the documents, hand the treaties back to her then ask, "How did you do that?"

Winlight says, "Sorry I time travel. I saw this event in times past."

They both laugh at that to and say, "That explains how you were so certain that we would agree with the treaties and why you greeted us as friends though we had never met, you are far strong."

Stella says, "Winlight."

Winlight faces her. Stella continues, "Only the ruler of a land has right to make treaties, as such you are now queen, being so much stronger than I am."

With tears flowing down her face Winlight says, "I am sorry mother."

Stella says, "Don't be. I am glad that you are so strong, and that I got to meet the one you love. Also see your first treaties."

They hug for a few moments then the leadership items are handed over and Stella walks out. I hurt for them. Winlight then has her first council meeting. A couple of months later, I see Winlight hide two children. One a pure spell caster, hidden with some humans and one that will rule after her, hidden with the tiger pack leader. While there Winlight asks the pack leader to not interfere with the soon to be events so its pack stays safe and alive. They agree.

One year later the council gathers again. The magic I can knowingly use at the next part of my test is mermaid, dragon, crystal, fairy, spell-caster, fire spinks, water spinks, sunbeam, moonbeam, elf, north-wind, and south-wind.

Major loss

When the council joins Winlight, they see her staff is glowing, so they know that she is using magic. When Winlight finishes using magic, she blinks and says, "The children that are your successors need to be hidden away from the magic lands. I have locked their magic until my heir comes home and becomes the ruler of this land. We are all in danger. It is important that the children do not live in the magic lands till the next Peacemaker rules as they would be killed too."

Winlight continues, "It saddens me much that the best I can do is to send them all away without being able to use their magic. The safety of our heirs ensures the safety of all the people, though many will be killed. No one should interfere with my death, for upon my death the seal on the children's magic will be complete. Only if they learn as no magic would they survive. It will be a long time before this land is as it is now, thriving with life, love, happiness, and peace. I do not expect that it will be very long before the event I saw happens. You are all dismissed."

The council all stare for a couple minutes then they leave, knowing that it is important to do as she says. They immediately do as Winlight told them. Two years later, everyone that was living in her magic lands and could be found is killed. Seeing so much life loss, I pass out. When I wake up, I find the next to rule my nation there, a boy. This boy is named Jack. When the fighting started, the tiger pack leader took Jack far away and left him near a human village. Some people there took a baby in and provided for him. He never used his magic. That is why it took me years to find him. He is married and his wife is expecting.

Months later, I see them have a girl. They name their daughter Lilly. She also does not use magic. When she grows up and gets married, she has a son. She names the boy Mao. I wonder if she cries much for the nation in her past that lost so many lives. I watch him grow up. His wife asks him to choose a name for their daughter. He lets her know he wants time to think before he chooses a name.

She agrees. Alone later that evening, he says, "Guardian boss, what should I name the daughter my wife and I are expecting?"

Zeffron shows up looking male saying, "Give her the honored name or initials that would be the honored name."

Mao nods. Zeffron leaves. The next day, Mao tells his wife, "I have decided to name our girl Sara Ann Marie Peacemaker."

His wife says, "Sara is a nice name. Why Peacemaker? It is not our last name."

Give her the last name Peacemaker

Mao says, "Yes dear it is. I never gave it up. I took your last name to stay safe, but I still have the last name Peacemaker. By giving it to our daughter I am declaring her birthright."

His wife asks, "What birthright? Why were you afraid for your safety to take my last name?"

Mao sighs, "My ancestors have been targeted for death. That is why I took your last name."

She interrupts, "Why give that last name to our girl since you are afraid to use it?"

Mao says, "I do as it is her birthright. It allows her to go to the place that her ancestors lived in as one of them. It gives her full access to everything her ancestors owned."

His wife asks, "Is it worth her safety?"

Mao says, "It is. Once she can defend herself, I will let her know what is special about the name."

She asks, "What is special about the name?"

Mao asks, "Do you know how to read maps?"

She asks, "What does that have to do with it?"

Mao says, "I will show you a map my ancestors did as they experienced locations through traveling. Perhaps then you would understand."

He spreads out a map. She says, "I do not recognize anything on the map."

Mao says, "That is because this is only a third of it. Let me pull out the second piece."

He does. After he spreads it out, she says, "This is the nation we live in."

Mao says, "Yes, it is. You see they are border nations on the maps."

She says, "Yes. What about it?"

Mao opens the third map and lines up the borders of the nations on the other side of the first map he opened. He asks, "Ready to see the rest of the map?"

She agrees. Mao unrolls the rest. She seems confused for a bit before questioning, "Your last name is a nation's name?"

Mao says, "That is right, Fray, it is. Our daughter has right to rule a nation if we give her the last name. It is my birthright, but I am not strong enough to lead the people. Sara might be, but without the name they will not allow her to no matter her strength. In giving her the name, we make her a princess. On my death, she becomes the ruler there or as I do, holds the position in a lock until one given the name is strong enough to lead them."

Fray asks, "You are a prince?"

Mao says, "My linage says I am. The people do not listen to me. I cannot rule but I am the only one in the bloodline until now. Sara might rule. If she is strong enough, she gains the throne. If she is not strong enough, she hides her identity as I have to so to stay safe and passes the right to any child, she one day has."

Fray asks, "What if she has more than one child? What if we have another child?"

Mao says, "More than one child is extremely rare in my family line. If we had another of if she has more than one, the strongest would gain right to inherit the throne. We need to move from here and get her closer to that nation. It is the best place for her."

They start packing. Mao handles all the heavy things, such as cooking equipment and utensils that are good for traveling. Fray handles the lightweight items, such as clothes and personal hygiene items. As they finish that a few days later, Fray asks, "What will we do when it gets close to time for Sara to be born?"

Mao replies, "We find a place to rest for a bit before we continue on. I think we should reach the second part of the map in three years after you have Sara. We should get to the nation my ancestors ruled by the time Sara is ten, pending any major occurrences."

They head out a few days later. Five years pass by as they travel toward the nation Sara will rule. Sara is four and walks by them at times but rides their cart more often, so they make better time. The woman has taken ill.

Though she tries to hide it, Mao's magic feels it. Mao says, "I think we should rest here for a few days. Sara needs social interaction. We should check in with the nation's king."

His wife says, "Alright."

They go to the castle. There Mao asks, "Sir King, my family and I are travelers. We were hoping to spend a few days here before continuing on. Might we?"

The king questions,, "Why do none of you bow?"

Mao says, "My family follows my example. I have never bowed to anyone. It was never how my parents acted, so I never do so."

The king asks, "You have a family history of disrespect?"

A child is alone

Mao replies, "No. We just show respect differently than most. We salute those we respect and only those we respect. If we salute, then you can know for sure that you have our respect and we would help you."

The king says, "Very well. You can stay as long as you need. Show them to some rooms."

His guards obey. Mao and his wife are given one room and Sara's room is across from theirs. They enter them. In the middle of the night I feel the loss of Mao's wife and minutes later, Mao. Sara runs out of her room and drops by their door crying. In that moment, I know her magic is strong enough to lead the people. A couple hours later, a guard comes over and says, "Sire invites you and your parents to join his family for breakfast."

Sara stands up saying, "Show me to them."

He says, "I must let your parents know."

Sara says, "You will not get any response."

He knocks on the door then calls out the message. After five minutes he leads Sara to the throne room. The king asks, "Do your parents not respect me enough to join my family for breakfast?"

Sara sighs, "I knew mom was not well. She tried to put off that she was, but I knew better. Dad, he has no will to live without her. They are dead."

The royal family, a few guards and Sara go to the room that Sara's parents were given. The door is locked. The king pounds on it asking than demanding they open the door. There is no response. After a half hour, he unlocks the door. Sara sighs, "They are dead."

Checking, the king has a doctor summoned. An hour later, the doctor pronounces them both dead. Sara says, "I told you they were."

The king asks, "How did you know? The room was locked, and you were outside of it. How did you know?"

Sara sighs, "I know my parents. So, I know when they are gone."

It is accepted. The king asks, "What do you intend to do now youth?"

Sara sighs, "If sir allows me to, I will live in his home serving him for a while in exchange for a place to sleep plus food to eat."

The king says, "That is fine."

His wife says, "I will get you some outfits to wear Sara, so you have change of clothes."

Sara says, "Thank you but I have clothes. In the room with my parents."

The queen says, "No, those things must be burned as there is no telling what has whatever they died from on it. Everything cloth gets burned and the rest must be sanitized before anyone else can use the room. All you have right now is what you have on."

Sara says, "Some clothes would help. Thank you for your kindness to me. Without it, I would be a homeless beggar for years as I am to young for many to hire me and I refuse to steal."

The queen takes her hand saying, "Let us go to the clothing store. I want to get you things you will actually wear, and I do not know your style."

Sara says, "Ommiad."

The queen asks, "What is that?"

Sara replies, "Sorry. My first language is difficult to translate. Mommy did not even understand it. I tend to speak it when unsure of how to act. I guess it would be close to thank you. I am not certain it translates as thank you, but it is used similarly."

The queen says, "Then we will go with that and I will say 'You are welcome.'"

They enter a clothes store. Sara asks, "How many outfits are you allowing me to have? Or what price limit?"

The queen says, "Pick out some you will wear. I will pay for up to thirty outfits. Do not worry about the cost. Remember that you said you would help my family, so pick at least some outfits suited for that."

Sara hugs her saying, "Ommiad."

The queen says, "You are welcome. Please pick out the clothes now."

Sara does so, picking out twenty-eight working outfits and two good dresses. She kept the cost down on all of them. After the queen confirms that is what Sara really wants, the clothes are paid for. They go back to the castle. Sara asks, "Where will I sleep here? Where are my meals to be had?"

The queen says, "Stay in the room you were allowed to use last night. You can join my family for meals."

Sara says, "No miss. I am a servant, where do the servants eat and sleep?"

The queen says, "Sara, you are young and alone. Your joining my family for all meals makes sure no one tries anything as we would know instantly if anything occurred. I have heard someone I respect use the term you use as thank you before meeting you. Let my family be kind to you."

Sara says, "Your taking me in is kindness enough."

The queen places her hand on Sara's shoulder whispering, "Keep the young one safe and healthy. Your parents introduced you in a tone of respect. I have met another that respected them but told me he had not met them. Sara, please let us help you."

Sara says, "Kind queen."

Heading home

With that they enter the room Sara was given. After they hang all the outfits in the wardrobe, they go down for lunch. Sara eats silently. Then she is shown to where she will work. Sara is placed under a woman supervisor and trained to mop the hallways. A few days later, Sara has mastered that and starts decreasing the time it takes her to complete it. A week later, Sara adds another task to her day. Two weeks after that, Sara learns another task. Soon she gets to eight tasks a day. Sara completes them all well. Ten years pass by there. Sara spends her days off helping the queen in her garden. The queen tells her often that she does not have to, but Sara always insists on doing so. Sara turns fifteen then Zeffron appearing female goes over to Sara while she is helping the queen in her garden. Zeffron says in magic common, "Young one, your peoples are hurting. They need you to return home."

Sara looks at Zeffron saying, "I am now old enough that I am safe. Thank you for visiting."

The day finishes out normally. As Sara approaches the room, she uses here I hear her whisper, "How am I going to let sir know? His family has been so kind to me, I ought not to want to leave. Nevertheless, I cannot ignore my peoples and their needs. It has been three-hundred years since the last one held the throne there after all. They deserve to be able to go home and use their skills safely again."

At lunch, a few days later, Sara is far quieter than she usually is. The king asks, "Why are you distracted Sara?"

No response. The king raises his voice asking again. Sara blinks then says, "I am sorry for being rude sir, I had not meant to be. I did not hear you. I am distracted as I am remembering."

The king asks, "Remembering?"

Sara answers, "Friends, I care about, and wondering how they are."

The king asks, "Do they live far from here?"

Sara replies, "I am not sure, I haven't seen them in years. I do not even know if they would remember me, I would enjoy finding out though. From what I last knew, the closest one on foot would be a year away."

The king says, "Well Sara, you have been very loyal to me from the day you came in this land ten years ago. I do not mind helping you now. It would take three months in a carriage. Me, my wife and youngest would take you if you do not mind us doing so. I would have my oldest son also, except someone needs to stay here to make sure things stay in order. Thank you for all the information you have gathered for my family over the years."

Sara says, "They know you are super busy so they would rather come to a commoner. It is easier for them to tell me. That keeps them from the legal hassle. Thank you for the offer of a ride. I will take it."

The king places his oldest son in charge early the next day and the four of them set out with some guards. Sara tells them what direction to head. Three months pass as they ride, stopping every night in a hotel. Then in the mid-afternoon Sara asks, "Stop please."

They are soon stopped. Sara gets out and goes over to the new dragon king. A girl slightly younger than Sara is. Sara says, "Greetings Diadon. I am Sara Ann Marie. Might my companions and I join your family for dinner?"

Diadon looks at Sara then says, "For sure miss. I feel as if I should know you, yet I do not recall ever meeting you before."

Sara says, "Do not worry about it. Let your parents know they have company coming for dinner."

Diadon nods and walks off. Sara goes back to the carriage. There Sara says, "We have all been invited to dinner. I have already accepted, and it would be very rude not to go."

The king says, "We will not be rude to them. Sara, next time ask me first before agreeing."

Sara says, "Very well sir. The girl waits to lead us to her home."

They follow Diadon at a much slower pace than they were going on the way to that town. I think I will pause my story here so you can keep up with it. I will pick up my story in *Tales of the Peacemaker: Years in Peace.*

www.ingramcontent.com/pod-product-compliance
Lightning Source LLC
Chambersburg PA
CBHW030636190726
48286CB00008B/2545